The Book
of
Atrocities

WOL-VRIEY

Burning Bulb
PUBLISHING

The Book
of
Atrocities

WOL-VRIEY

Burning Bulb
PUBLISHING

The Book of Atrocities
By **Wol-vriey**

Burning Bulb Publishing
P.O. Box 4721
Bridgeport, WV 26330-4721
United States of America
www.BurningBulbPublishing.com

Cover photo by Joanne Adela Low from Pexels.
Author Photo: Lolade Akinsowon © 2014.

First Edition.

Paperback Edition ISBN: 978-1-948278-24-9

Printed in the United States of America

Art/Entertainment is never useless,
Because all art is medicine.
Artists/Entertainers are the doctors of the soul.

CHAPTER 1

Liz

On that Saturday evening, they arrived at the house just as the sun was setting. It was late summer, mid-August, and even though the day had been mostly warm, the wind this evening was chilly, as if announcing the coming change in season.

The house itself was on Carver Street, which was up in the northwestern part of Raynham. Lots of trees surrounded the building, though it was still visible from the road as Melody Melville turned her brown BMW SUV into the long driveway.

"Why on earth did Drake buy this out-of-the-way place?" Liz Melville asked as the SUV rolled over the wide concrete strip towards the waiting building. "I'd have thought properties in Boston were more his speed now?"

Melody took her eyes off the wheel for a second and looked over at Liz, who was seated beside her in the front passenger seat. She smiled coolly. "Oh, you know how Drake is. Once he gets an idea in his head, that's it. Nothing anyone says can make him change his mind. Someone brought us here to look at this place and once he saw it he wanted it. He said it had an aura that he liked."

An aura he liked? Yeah, that definitely sounds like Drake. Liz nodded back at Melody and then shivered. Oh, she knew exactly what the other woman meant.

All at once, the fear she'd been repressing since yesterday morning filled her again. Suddenly, the space inside the SUV seemed to be shrinking, like it would crush all of them to a mangled and bleeding pulp. She felt like screaming at her fellow travelers to leap out of the vehicle.

And then her panic passed. She felt calm again. She reminded herself that she'd just imagined everything; that she'd been hungover at the time and . . . and . . .

But there's no point in lying to myself. I have no proper explanation for what happened yesterday.

She said nothing else while Melody parked the car, instead turning to look at her friend Bonnie, who was seated in the backseat. Bonnie was rooting through her handbag for something—most likely a fresh cigarette pack. Bonnie chain-smoked like an ancient locomotive.

Bonnie looked bored. Liz had insisted that she come along on this trip and Bonnie had grudgingly agreed. At first though, she'd utterly refused to travel from Dayton, Ohio to Raynham, Massachusetts, saying she had to clean her apartment, until Liz had explained that Melody would be driving, at which statement Bonnie had immediately said she was coming along too, so she could protect Liz.

Liz hadn't thought too much about what that meant then. At the time she'd been desperate for Bonnie's company. The woman was her best friend. But now those words came back and haunted her:

What exactly is it that Bonnie wants to protect me from?

No time to ponder that however.

"Alright, guys, out of the car!" Melody chirpily announced.

The three of them got out and stood by the vehicle for a moment and stared at the house which they'd driven across three states to arrive at.

We're admittedly a weird trio, Liz thought, looking her companions over. *A missing bestselling author's ex-wife, his current wife, and the ex-wife's best friend. Two casually dressed women with long black hair; and blonde Bonnie, who, in that short blue dress and high heels, looks like she's attending a dance.*

Bonnie Pierson was trashy, there was no doubt about that. Bonnie was also the tallest of their trio at five foot eight inches. Liz was five foot four, Melody five foot too. Age-wise, all three of them were in their early thirties.

Bonnie flipped a cigarette from her pack and lit up. Melody pulled a comb from her purse and expertly fixed her hair without the aid of a mirror; this was her automatic response once there were members of the press nearby.

Liz turned her attention to the house. It was a normal enough construction for this northeast part of the country: two extra-wide stories with lots of windows, and with an equally wide screened-off front porch. Gray and white paint mostly, though the gray looked faded, like the building hadn't yet been renovated. There was a garage on the right side of the house, in which a blue Ford sedan was parked.

Add in a swing for pre-teen kids and a couple of SUVs and this is just the sort of place that a normal, hard working and respectable middle-class American family would live in, Liz thought with apprehension. *Which is what scares me, because my ex-husband isn't interested in such places. If Drake's gonna buy a place as a hideaway, it's gonna be some crumbling gothic mansion that gives you the creeps the moment you see it. But this place looks more normal that normal itself.*

That fact made her really suspicious of the house. Knowing Drake Melville like she did, this building's seeming normalcy had to be a façade. The good thing however, was that her panic didn't return. This current fear she felt was merely a fear of the unknown. Along with her fear of her ex-husband himself, whom she'd long suspected of being allied to forces she wanted no dealings with.

And if that's the case, why on earth am I coming to meet him here? But the answer to that's quite simple, right? Hey, I'm scared of what he might unleash on me if I didn't come?

Which made more sense than accepting that maybe she was still in love with the sonofabitch and just wanted to see him again.

"Weird that Drake asked you two to meet him *here*," Bonnie said between one puff of cigarette smoke and another.

Glad of the distraction from her thoughts and fears, Liz corrected her bestie: "Nah, he ain't here. We're meeting a guy here who'll take us all to meet with Drake. If Drake *was* living here I think the neighbors would have noticed him ages ago."

"But hey, don't you two think this is rather mysterious anyway?" Bonnie asked.

Melody laughed, a pleasant if strained sound. "When your husband's been missing for three whole years," she said, "mystery more or less becomes your daily routine." She stopped speaking for a moment to tap on the screen of her iPhone. "Particularly when he keeps sending me text message that AT&T can't trace the source of."

"Hey, *I* never got any of those from him," Liz said without thinking; then she realized why before Melody also enlightened her with a catty smile:

"But you're *divorced* from him, honey," Melody Melville pointed out. "It's not like you ever chatted with him since your parting about anything other than your kid Frankie, is it? And even in that situation, I don't think Drake was the world's most interested father before he went missing."

Liz nodded sourly at that. Her ex had never even requested shared custody of their son.

"Well, we can't stay out here forever," Melody said after a glance heavenward. "The sky's getting darker by the minute and those inside are certain to have heard us pull up outside the house. Which means they'll be wondering what's keeping us outside. Might as well knock on the door."

"Someone's coming to the door," Bonnie said as they pushed open the screen door and stepped up off the stairs onto the front porch.

The front door had an inset window of frosted glass at about face-height. Liz noticed the human shadow behind the partition, and then the door opened and . . .

Liz immediately recognized the man who opened the front door, even though she'd never met or seen him before. And, judging from their startled gasps, so did her two companions.

All three women quickly stepped back from the unexpected apparition. They only stopped retreating when the walls of the porch screen hit them in the back. They'd have retreated back to their SUV, but were too surprised to locate the screen door behind them.

"Are-are-are you S-S-S-S-Seer J-J-Jonah?" Bonnie finally blurted out when she found her voice.

"Yes I am," the man replied with an amused smile. "And you three ladies are welcome to Mr. Melville's little hideaway."

"Oh, so he is here then?" Liz asked. "He's inside the house?"

The strange man shook his head. "No, Mr. Drake is not here at the moment, but as promised, you three will be escorted by me to meet him tomorrow morning."

Liz nodded, while still trying to get her head around the fact that she was meeting in the flesh the main character from her ex-husband's infamous novel *The Bleeding Oysters*.

'Seer Jonah,' supposedly so named because, although called to be a prophet of God and trained and ordained as a priest, he'd chosen to turn away from God to practice his own sexual and magical version of religion, was possibly the most evil man who'd ever lived. A man without morals of any sort; a man for whom performing the most heinous of wickednesses and witchcrafts was like a dog drinking water or a politician kissing a baby. Drake's book *The Bleeding Oysters* was the fictional epic saga of Seer Jonah's quest for personal enlightenment and godhood, in which murder, mutilation, torture, rape, and a slew of disgusting magical rituals were the order of the day; most of these heinous acts committed by Jonah himself.

And now to meet this horrible person in the flesh? With the implied suggestion that what the world had so far considered fiction might be fact?

This had been the cause of their instinctive retreat on recognizing him. And there was no mistaking that he was the one—either that, or he was some obsessed fan of Drake Melville's work (or an employee?) who had had himself tattooed to match the novel's description.

Liz was an actress; she was used to fans cosplaying movie characters that she'd acted. But this?

In keeping with the character in *The Bleeding Oysters*, this 'Seer Jonah' was a slim man of average height. His eyes were gray. His nose was long and thin, his lips thin and cruel, his smile cruel yet sensual. His skin was very pale. There was no telling how old he was—he could be anywhere between thirty and fifty.

He was bald, with strange red words tattooed on his head. Liz could tell that the words were an ancient script, but had no idea what they meant. And, clearest of all, this 'Seer Jonah' had 'I WILL SAVE YOU' tattooed in black above both of his eyes in place of his eyebrows, and also tattooed across his upper lip in place of a mustache. His open short-sleeved shirt and shorts let them see that his body was decorated with more of the same indecipherable red writing that covered his head. He seemed to be completely hairless.

He looked exactly like Drake's fictional character. Handsome and seeming to reek perversion.

"But are you the *real* Seer Jonah?" Melody asked, recovering her composure. "You're just an employee of my husband's that he's paid to dress up like this, aren't you?"

The man laughed. "A good question. But then, ask yourself—is Seer Jonah real? If he's fictional, how can I be him? And if he's real; can anyone be that monstrous?"

Melody pondered on that.

"You're not going to tell us, are you?" Liz asked after a few moments when nothing more was said by anyone. She both disliked and distrusted this tattooed man. She could sense his aura and it was dark and completely unpleasant—'sleazy' didn't even begin to describe what she sensed about him. (Liz Melville's only relief, and what firmed her conviction that *The Bleeding Oysters* was fiction, was the fact that the novel took place in an alternate Earth, one where magic had made the world stop spinning and where the sun never moved from its fixed position in the sky.)

Seer Jonah smiled at her. "You decide." He nodded towards Melody. "Mrs. Melville thinks I'm one of her husband's employees. Which I might be. But you, you must make up your own mind about me. Am I real or a fake?"

Liz shrugged. "So this is another of Drake's mind games? Oh brother, don't tell me I'm in for that spooky crap again." Then she smiled coolly at their host. "Okay, two can play that game then. Dude, I'm with Melody on this. You're a fake, an employee of Drake's."

"Fair enough," the tattooed man replied.

He was clearly about to say more when Bonnie interrupted: "Hey, everyone, now that the introductions are made, can we just step inside? My feet are killing me, standing here like this."

Seer Jonah nodded. "Yes, of course. Please come inside, all of you. It was wrong of me to keep you out here for so long. The others are waiting to greet you."

CHAPTER 2

Chloe

Chloe Melville looked up from her phone as the two women who shared her surname entered the living room. Her brother's two wives were followed by a woman she'd not met before, a tall blonde who trailed cigarette smoke like exhaust fumes.

The three women strode into the room and waved greetings at Chloe and her two companions.

Chloe grinned back. "Hi, Liz . . . Melody."

"I'm Bonnie Pierson," the third woman introduced herself. "Tagging along to keep Liz safe."

There was some laughter at that and Melody rolled her eyes.

"Todd Wilson . . . Nick Sinclair," Chloe's own two companions introduced themselves, nodding from their seats.

As a casual observer would quickly deduce from the external size of the house, its interior was quite spacious. The living room was wide and roomy. It had large windows with pale drapes patterned with black and red flowers. Adjoining the living room on its western side was an equally large dining room extension. A doorway led off from the dining room into the kitchen, from where currently came tantalizing odors of cooking food. Opposite the dining room, beside the short hallway that led into the eastern depths of the house, a spiral stairway rose to the upper floor.

Chloe, Nick, and Todd were seated with their backs to the dining room. The TV was on but with the volume turned down. The headline story was about a visit by the First Lady to a war veteran's hospital in Missouri, while a scrolling ribbon at the bottom of the screen noted that the Massachusetts State Police were still looking for the psycho nicknamed 'Insane Jane.'

Being journalists, none of the three of them felt any need to hear what the reporters were saying. Todd was the only one of them who actually seemed to be paying attention to the activities onscreen, and even this was only during the short periods between him sucking on his cigarette, those interludes when he tapped ash into a ghoulish brass ashtray designed in the shape of a human skull with the top cut off.

Seer Jonah walked in from the foyer and gestured around at the empty armchairs. "Please seat yourselves, ladies." Then he gestured to the drinks cabinet in the corner. "And while you all get properly acquainted, can I pour you something to drink?"

"Johnnie Walker Black," Bonnie immediately replied. "Lots of it."

He nodded and looked enquiringly at Liz and Melody.

"Same as Bonnie," Liz said. "I need something to dull my suspicions."

Melody thought for a moment. "Coffee or I'm bound to fall asleep while sitting here. I've been up since 4 a.m."

Seer Jonah strode over to the drinks cabinet and took down glasses from a shelf. "I'm cooking dinner," he said over his shoulder, explaining the tantalizing odor of roasting meat to the new arrivals. "Steak. It'll be ready in about ten minutes."

Chloe watched him, staring at the red lines of text that ran around his legs. Each slim leg was tattooed in what seemed a continuous red loop, with maybe an inch of spacing between the lines. What was visible of the rest of him—his arms and head; seemingly everywhere except his face—was similarly decorated, with the tattoos on his head spiraling up from the back of his neck to end in a red circle at the exact center of his scalp. And then there were those crazy 'I WILL SAVE YOU' tattoos he had instead of eyebrows and mustache.

Oh, Chloe found Seer Jonah extremely creepy. If her older brother hadn't texted her very specific instructions as to how to contact him, and those instructions hadn't specifically mentioned that she'd meet this man here, she'd be out of here already and halfway back to Boston.

Nick, who was seated on her immediate left, leaned over and whispered in her ear: "Girl, that's one really weird dude. He really does seem capable of doing the kinda sick shit that made your brother's book so popular. You sure you wanna go through with this, Chloe?"

She turned to Nick, shrugged, and whispered back: "We've no choice. Drake said to come here and we'd meet this guy, who'd lead us to him. We'll just have to wait and see what happens."

Nick shrugged too. He sank back into his chair and sipped from his glass of wine. Nick Sinclair was dark, handsome, and in his early-thirties. An ex-boyfriend of hers. Like Chloe, Nick too was a correspondent for the Boston Globe, here to assist her in recording what would most likely be the literary scoop of the year. Missing bestselling author Drake Melville suddenly resurfaces again with his new novel. Oh, that story was going to sell beyond everyone's wildest dreams.

And we've exclusive coverage. She grinned. *Of course, that's because I'm Drake's sister.*

Chloe felt very nervous, like giant moths were circling candles in her belly. Her apprehension wasn't just because she was about to see her brother after so long, but also because of the interview she would conduct with him.

This was her big break and she wasn't prepared to either screw it up herself, or let anyone else screw it up for her.

And the paper aren't taking any chances either, she thought grimly. *That's why they sent Nick along with me. Which isn't too bad.*

In fact, now that Chloe Melville had met the previously believed-to-be-fictional Seer Jonah in person, she was glad that Nick was here with her.

Oh, but he has to be a fake. Another of Drake's jokes. If he's the real deal, he's guilty of so many crimes that he'd be locked up forever. This dude has to be the worst and sickest psycho in world history; he makes Hitler look like an apprentice serial killer. In Drake's novel, Seer Jonah actually believes he can force God to accept people into Heaven by hurting them so badly that the Almighty will have pity on them. But . . . no, that's just fiction. This guy didn't in the least bit mind Todd filming him after we arrived, so he can't be a criminal.

She looked at Todd, who was sitting beyond Nick on her far left, a cigarette between his lips. Todd Wilson was a rugged and muscular man in his mid-forties. He'd been a US Marine, had served in both Iraq and Afghanistan. After leaving the army, Todd had returned to the battlefront as a war video correspondent, before two bullets in the gut had forced him to return home again.

She nodded. Their features editor Shelly Martin had known what she was doing, sending these two men along with her. Where Nick was resourceful and naturally inquisitive, Todd Wilson was tougher than diamonds. If you planned a fuck-up, you tried to do it away from Todd's vicinity.

So I shouldn't feel worried for my safety now. Todd's packing a gun. All I gotta do is spend the night here, and in the morning follow this weirdo across town to meet my brother and hear his explanation of how he's somehow hidden himself from the world for the past three years. Oh yeah, and there's the scoop on his new novel too. I'm supposed to collect that and bear it to Chaos House . . .

Seer Jonah was just handing Melody and Liz their drinks. Chloe's gaze had strayed to watching the settling darkness outside the living room windows, but now she studied Drake's wives instead. She and her brother had always been very close, confiding in each other about everything, and so she knew a lot about the two women.

Both were about the same height and had glossy black hair, but there the similarities between them ended. Liz was slim and Melody a little plump. Liz had blue eyes and the suspicious thin-lipped face of a woman who thought life was out to get her. Melody's eyes were dark and she had a large generous-lipped mouth; she also seemed happier than Liz did. Both were dressed the same—in jeans and tee-shirts, but despite Melody having more money, Liz's clothes seemed to fit her better.

Chloe had always found the hair/eye color contrast between Drake and his wives intriguing, because she and he were both blondes with light-brown eyes.

Liz noticed Chloe staring at her and grinned back. "Strange gathering tonight, right? Three women all with the same surname here to meet the same runaway man."

"Haha, you're so right." Melody slapped her thigh and sipped her coffee.

Chloe laughed too and nodded. *But you ran away first,* she couldn't help thinking at Liz.

To her as a reporter, Liz leaving Drake was one of the world's big mysteries. As far as Chloe knew, back then the pair had been blissfully happy. And then one day, Liz had just upped and left; she'd packed all her stuff, taken the baby and run off. Chloe had asked Drake what they'd fought over. He'd replied that they hadn't fought; said he was as puzzled as herself as to why the woman he deeply loved had deserted him. She'd suspected that there was more to it than that, but hadn't pressed the case. She figured he'd tell her the whole story when he felt ready.

Chloe stole a glance at Melody. Drake hadn't remarried until he was famous. He'd had a few flings with actresses and rock stars, most notably with Janet Orgasm, lead singer of rock supergroup Slain Jane. Shortly after breaking up with Jane O, he'd met Melody at a book party in New York and had been immediately smitten with her. So smitten in fact that it hadn't mattered that Melody Kaye was a transsexual.

Chloe surreptitiously stared at her sister-in-law, concentrating her gaze on the area of blue denim fabric at the crotch of Melody's jeans. Trying to spot the bulge made by the woman's penis and testicles was a game she often played with herself whenever they were alone together. So far she'd not won once; she was still amazed at how something that was so prominent when aroused could be hidden so well as to be indiscernible when it wasn't sexually swollen with blood.

Intrigued by the sexual possibilities, she'd asked her brother who played the man in the sack. He'd laughed and told her Melody was totally passive in bed; he was the one doing all the humping and pumping, not she.

"You know me, sis," he'd said. "No way I'm letting anyone stick anything up my butt. My ass is an exit, not an entrance."

Chloe suddenly felt startled. She was surprised to find herself thinking about sex. This was unusual for her. She disliked thinking about sex; she had so much unpleasant sexual baggage she needed to ditch. Most times the mere suggestion of two naked people in a bed made her feel like puking.

And I'm not drunk either. She'd only had the one glass of wine; her empty glass now stood on the coffee table in front of her. Seer Jonah had offered to refill it, but she'd declined the offer. He'd left the bottle on the coffee table though. She stared at it; its red content half drunk away. *Maybe before bed, to help me sleep.*

But then she decided that maybe it wasn't so unusual that she was thinking about sex tonight. *There are three men and four women present in this house, and except for Melody, who's still married to Drake, and Todd—both of whom are wearing wedding rings—everyone else here is single, including the new girl Bonnie. Five single people raises all kinds of mating possibilities for one night stands. And the way Bonnie keeps looking at Jonah and Liz, I think she's getting ready for a threesome. Weird how the suggestion of danger turns some people on.*

And then there was her anticipation of seeing her brother again after all this while. *I'm sure everyone else shares my excitement—well, everyone except Todd, who never gets excited about anything.*

Nick's behavior seemed to confirm her one-night-stand theory. He wasn't paying much attention to her. Chloe felt amused; her ex-boyfriend seemed to be doing his best to catch Bonnie's attention, while for her own part the tall blonde chain-smoked away and did her best to ignore Nick. And then Seer Jonah looked at Bonnie and she seemed to both expand and shrivel under his gaze.

What's the deal with her, I wonder?

"I need to check on the roast," Seer Jonah informed them and left for the kitchen.

Once he'd left them Bonnie instantly leaned over and whispered something in Liz's ear that made Liz giggle and whisper back. Then Bonnie sat back looking pleased with herself.

Chloe was still trying to figure out the strange dynamic between Liz and Bonnie, when Nick leaned over and whispered in her own ear: "The blonde wants to fuck your brother's ex, but apparently Liz hasn't realized it yet. Or maybe she does and is playing hard to get. Or she doesn't want to be gotten."

Chloe felt scandalized. "Huh? Nick you can't be serious!"

"Oh, I am. Watch what happens after dinner, as in who pairs off with who at bedtime."

"How can you be certain?"

He laughed. "Because I like Bonnie myself. I'd like to hook up with her, but she's been making a point of not noticing me trying to catch her eye."

"C'mon, her not liking you doesn't make her a lesbian!" Chloe was taking care to keep her voice down.

"Yeah, yeah, I know that," Nick quickly agreed. "But she's also been taking every chance she gets to touch Liz, brushing her fingers against her arm and thigh. Look how she's leaning against her now, and just now, when she whispered to her . . . it looked like it was taking our dear Bonnie all of her self-control not to lick Liz's ear." Nick laughed. "So I've clearly struck out there, but it looks like Liz is about getting lucky tonight, though she doesn't realize it yet."

"Hey, she's been staring at our host too."

Nick laughed some more. "Aw, the woman's just scared stiff of him. And not in a stiff-dick way."

Still laughing, he turned to ask Todd something.

For distraction, with Liz either too tired to talk or not willing to say anything, Melody had taken to staring at the TV like Todd was doing. Bonnie lit a fresh cigarette, then, as if they'd started off a smoking contest, Todd did too. Nick poured himself another glass of wine; Chloe shook her head when he gestured to her wineglass.

Chloe was wondering how to start up a general conversation, when Seer Jonah walked through the dining room.

"Dinner's ready, folks, please come to the dining table."

And so they all got up and went to eat.

CHAPTER 3

Liz

Dinner was a lively enough affair.

Seer Jonah was a fine host, serving everybody the hot sizzling steaks from the oven, along with spaghetti and sauce, fries and more wine; and then sitting down and tucking in with the rest of them.

As though it had been planned from the offset, Melody, Liz and her best friend were seated on one side of the dining table and Drake's sister and her companions on the other side. It was a large table, big enough even for Jonah to sit beside Bonnie, whom he occasionally joked with. Bonnie seemed unsure whether to be flattered or repulsed by his attentions. She looked like she wanted to cool him off but at the same time didn't desire to offend him. She also looked scared, which Liz could definitely relate to, because Seer Jonah scared her too.

Bonnie's clear discomfort made Liz grin. It seemed like Seer Jonah would be taking her amorous bestie off of her hands, at least for tonight.

Oh yes, unknown to Nick and Chloe, Liz *had* noticed their short vocal interchange. By lip-reading Nick's lips, she'd also caught some of what he'd said.

So Bonnie's in love with me? Bonnie wants to have sex with me?

Liz could hardly believe it. *Oh no,* she thought, *how could I ever have been so blind? I thought we were just friends.*

But now, it all came back to her, how Bonnie was always hugging and touching her on the slightest of pretexts, and also looking at her in that questioning way, as if . . . well, Liz had never known how exactly to interpret those glances, but she did now and really wished she didn't.

Oh my dear God, what the hell do I do now that my best friend wants to eat my pussy?

For a few seconds she wallowed in her confusion, feeling a slight excitement, an awakening of desire, pleasure tingling in her crotch. She let herself imagine what it would be like lying naked together with Bonnie in a bed with cool sheets, a midsummer night's breeze blowing in through the open windows and caressing both of their skins.

It was a pleasant image to consider, and as she thought on it she looked up at Bonnie. As if sensing the sudden connection between them, Bonnie smiled back at her. And this time, after all the time they'd spent together as best friends, Elizabeth Melville finally saw the desire in Bonnie's eyes, that wanting to be more than just friends.

And then, just like that, her desire to make love to Bonnie vanished.

No, Liz's desire didn't drain from her like water through a sieve, nor did it evaporate like oil fumes from a hot skillet. Instead, her fledgling desire to lie in her best friend's arms and kiss and caress her suddenly switched over to her other sexual interest, one which she was only now admitting to herself.

Because, despite the suspicion and barely concealed animosity expected between two successive wives of the same man, two women who were both in love with him, Liz suddenly desired to fuck Melody Melville instead.

She wasn't sure when this desire of hers had begun. She liked to think it had started just yesterday morning when Melody had unexpectedly turned up at her doorstep. But thinking back, she suddenly realized that this desire to have sex with her successor in Drake's affections had been simmering in her loins for a long time.

She had no idea of Melody's feelings on the matter: was the transsexual woman similarly attracted to her, or was this just a one-sided thing?

She sneaked a glance at Melody. The woman's similarly long and jet-black hair gave Liz a fleeting impression—an illusion, she knew—that Drake had married Melody Kaye on an impulse, because he was still in love with *her*. It was a flattering thought that her missing husband might still be pining for her, and one that filled her with a sudden rush of desperation to see him.

But first, she had her replacement in his marital bed to deal with, in a sexual way.

She watched Melody from the corner of her eye, noticing the transsexual woman's graceful motions as she cut up her steak and lifted it to her mouth, the sensual curve of her lips as the food passed between them and then the calm but equally beautiful and perfect movement of her cheeks, jaws and throat as she chewed and swallowed.

Melody showed no sign that she was aware of Liz's scrutiny. When she looked up from her food and noticed Liz observing her, she merely smiled back at her and said, "This steak sure tastes great, don't it?"

"Huh?" Lost in her thoughts, Liz had temporarily forgotten her own food. Now she once more became aware of its delicious smell and realized she was hungry too.

She nodded back at Melody. "Yeah, it's really great." Then she smiled at Seer Jonah, who was sipping from a glass of water. "You're a really good cook," she told him.

"Thank you," he replied with a cool smile.

Liz still found the tattooed man creepy, but she was getting used to him now.

Melody had meanwhile returned her own attention to her food. Liz once more looked at Bonnie, wondering what would happen tonight if the two of them suddenly found themselves alone; although with the interest Seer Jonah was showing in her bestie, that seemed unlikely.

Now that she knew of her friend's desire for her, even with her own lust for Melody's touch and caresses, Liz felt it would be impossible to predict her own reaction if Bonnie were to suddenly grab and kiss her. *Will I melt into her arms or flee her feminine charms?* A melodramatic thought for sure, but she was an actress after all and melodrama was her life. In a sense she was always on stage.

She glanced once more at Bonnie's bony face, and then looked at the others seated around the dinner table. Everyone else was eating like they'd been starving all day; Chloe in particular.

Not wanting to be the odd woman out, Liz began eating too. As she sliced up her steak and twirled spaghetti and cheese sauce on her fork, fresh erotic images raged about her mind, spinning through her head like agitated birds.

She saw herself pinned down beneath Melody while the other woman trust her hard penis deep into her body, tantalizing her with pleasure. Then the perspective inverted and she saw herself riding Melody, with her hands pressing down the other woman's white-as-snow shoulders and then slithering over her sweat-slicked skin to grab and squeeze Melody's plump breasts. And all this while her own buttock cheeks were being parted wide by Melody's strong and yet delicate feminine fingers, with their fingernails digging into the soft pink flesh of each ass cheek as her transsexual lover's stiff and throbbing manhood (or should that rather be her hard and throbbing *womanhood?*) plunged deep as the ocean into her wet and dripping sexual canal, pumping her and satisfying her until both their ships of passion were wrecked on the shore by violent waves of orgasm.

"Hey c'mon, give us a hint, man," Chloe suddenly said, after setting down her glass of water, her question directed at their tattooed host. "Where exactly is Drake hiding? I mean it's like crazy, how he could go missing for three whole years and no one, not even his phone company, can tell where he is."

"Yeah," Todd agreed, "I've been trying to get my head around that for ages now. It don't make no sense how a man can just vanish like that. What is Drake using, huh? Has he got some custom-built gizmo blocking his signal? I mean his phone signal."

Liz nodded at the question. She'd been wondering the same thing forever now. How could anyone just completely vanish from sight in these modern times when the government tracked everything you did. As far as Liz knew, Uncle Sam could track you via the internet, via your credit cards and purchases, and via CCTV cameras and other devices either you or they owned. In short, with the way the world was wired now, this modern world of hyper-computerized multimedia insanity, how was it even possible for one of the world's most famous authors (or infamous authors, if you preferred that description) to vanish without a single trace for so long?

This was something else that scared Liz: knowing as she did the other strange things about her ex-husband, which she suspected no one else here had a clue about, not even his new wife or his sister.

Now Liz really began to question the wisdom of her coming here. Watching Seer Jonah flirt with Bonnie, a chill ran down her spine.

***

Ever since yesterday morning Liz had been in a state of tension. And even now her nerves quivered involuntarily each time she remembered how she'd embarked on this seemingly crazy quest.

She . . . she attacked her food, taking out her frustrations on it, occasionally looking up when someone else at the table made a witty comment. Most of these comments came from Seer Jonah, like when, wreathed in Bonnie's blue cigarette smoke, he asked her at what age she'd started smoking, because Bonnie, who was still both nervous and flattered by the tattooed man's attentions, kept lighting up cigarette after cigarette all through dinner, tapping out the ash and discarding the used-up butts into the creepy skull-shaped brass ashtray, which she was sharing with Todd.

Liz no longer knew what to make of it all.

Everyone's just chatting away, she thought, *as if being here is the most natural thing in the world. But I clearly sense that it isn't. I feel weird, so damn weird, like I know something bad is waiting to happen to us all, and my apprehension seems close to killing me. Oh, but maybe I'm just exaggerating again.*

At that moment a phone rang. It turned out to be Todd's. After pulling it from his pocket and glancing at the screen, he grinned at the others, pushed his chair back from the table, and stood up.

"It's my wife and kids," he explained. "I'll be right back." Leaving his dinner half-eaten, he walked off to take the call.

His leaving them reminded Liz that she too needed to make a phone call to her father. So she pushed back her own chair and also got to her feet.

"I'll be right back too," she told the others and then strode off out of the dining room, walked through the living room and out into the entrance foyer.

There by the front door, her intention to call her father was momentarily interrupted by her fresh impressions about this house. Yes, at first she'd thought there was something strange about Drake making this purchase. This house had seemed too ordinary to interest him, but, now that she was alone, without everyone else's psychic interference (though not into the New Age scene or paranormal encounters, this was the only way she could think of it), Liz felt that she sensed something unworldly about this place. As she leaned against the foyer wall and pulled her phone from her purse, she couldn't shake the feeling of oddity that this house, innocent as it seemed both outside and inside, created in her.

This is a very weird place, she thought with a shiver. *It's definitely unusual in some way. Which of course explains why Drake bought it.*

Then she shrugged off her unease and called her father.

He answered on the second ring.

"Hi, dad," she said, trying to sound as bright as she could so as not to alarm him. "Sorry I'm just calling you. I plumb forgot in the excitement of our arrival here."

"Hi, honey, how was your trip to Massachusetts?"

"Oh, it was fine," she replied. "We arrived here about an hour ago and have been trying to settle in."

"Any news of Drake yet?"

"Not yet, we're going to see him tomorrow morning. Hey, is Frankie still awake?"

"Yeah, the kid is watching Bugs Bunny. You wanna talk to him? Should I call him over?"

"Don't bother, I'll see him tomorrow evening. Just tell him I love him for me before you put him to bed."

"Will do, sweets." Her father's voice now grew concerned. "Hey, Lizbeth, you sure you're ok? You sound worried."

"No. I mean, yes, I'm fine," she replied quickly. "Nothing's wrong. I'm just tired out from our long trip."

"Yeah, well, a good night's sleep should fix that. Try to get to bed early. Okay, hon, gotta go. Frankie is signaling wildly to me about something—likely the damn cartoon rabbit has just got shot again."

"Alright, dad. Love you, see you tomorrow evening."

She hung up the call but didn't yet leave the foyer. She felt pleased. Speaking to her father had relaxed her. Talking to him had made her suspicions and her worries seem less plausible.

Somewhere deep in the house she heard Todd laughing on the phone with his family.

The man's unfeigned expression of joy soured Liz's good mood. Had she been selfish on the phone, thinking only of herself?

Maybe I should have spoken to Frankie, she thought. But then she shook her head. *No, not tonight.*

At the moment, speaking to she and Drake's autistic offspring would do her no good. And besides, Frankie wouldn't have appreciated being dragged away from his favorite cartoons. Her son loved his cartoons and, if she'd interrupted him, would have begun sulking, which would have made her aged father's job of looking after him that more difficult. Her father was a widower and had bad arthritis that made getting around difficult for him, so leaving Frankie with him for even one night was quite an imposition; but Frankie's regular caregiver Mrs. Bergman had called in sick this morning and Liz had had no alternative but to leave the kid with her dad instead.

A fresh chill ran down her spine. *How did Drake know about that?*

Drake, Drake, Drake. Yes, she was long divorced from him, but it seemed as if the ghost of their marriage continued to haunt her, not just in the physical presence of their mentally-challenged son, but in tiny, less apparent ways.

As Liz walked back to the dining room to join the others, she could not help but wonder about her strange marriage to Drake Melville.

***

Elizabeth Mary Turner had married Drake before he'd become somebody. Back then the only attraction he'd had for her was that he made her laugh. But had he actually made her laugh, or had she been laughing at him? At how funny and conceited he was? Because Drake had insisted he'd be a bestselling author when he'd been drowning in rejections from publishers; everyone had rejected his manuscripts.

It was a question she'd never been able to answer. Couldn't then, and still couldn't. Maybe she never would have an answer to it.

Anyway, whatever the reason for her liking him back then, she'd married him.

After the wedding they'd moved into a little bungalow in the Dayton, Ohio neighborhood of Five Oaks. It was a nice house, the sort of place that Drake claimed a writer could truly write in, even if he have no money.

The rent was low and their expectations as high as the clouds. But they were in love and happy and in that state of bliss nothing else mattered.

Alright, so the new bride's husband had always professed an interest in the arcane and esoteric. He'd owned a few volumes on magical lore that he said were necessary for his book research (Drake had been writing thrillers then). It had never gone further than that. His sister Chloe had told Liz that his interest in the occult went back to his adolescent years, but even then had never amounted to anything disturbing.

But now the craziness had begun. Weird voices in the night. Weird happenings too. Things that scared the crap out of Liz. On several occasions she'd caught Drake talking to no one . . . There'd been no one in the room when she'd walked in, despite the fact that she'd heard voices replying him.

Once, on entering their living room at midnight after hearing a female voice replying her husband's, she'd found an extra wineglass on the coffee table. The scary thing was that the wine in the extra glass was still sloshing about, as if the glass had been set down in a hurry. But there had been no one else in the house.

When the weirdness had threatened to snap her sanity, Liz had taken their baby son Frankie and had gotten out. Ran off one night and never returned. Once certain she was safe from her husband and his invisible friends, she'd filed for divorce. She'd been angered that Drake never contested the divorce. Was he as relieved to be rid of her as she was to be free of him?

This of course, had all happened before he'd published *The Bleeding Oysters*. When the book became a sensation, she'd sued Drake for child support. Before then, there had been no point to a lawsuit: she'd been earning more than he was.

He'd not contested the lawsuit; had in fact given her more money than she'd requested.

She'd never put two-and-two together though and realized that it was right after she'd gotten the first child support payment that Frankie had begun acting weird—had suddenly developed his mental deficiencies.

Drake had never come to see Frankie. Not once. He'd begun behaving like the boy didn't exist. Liz had hated him for that.

***

After their marriage ended, Liz had kept Drake's surname. It had seemed natural to do so at the time, as she hadn't stopped loving him.

In addition, even though her acting career had begun showing signs of getting off the ground with some work in a few commercials and TV serials, she wasn't well-known enough to bother reverting back to her maiden name.

In retrospect however, even though unintended, this decision of hers (or lack of one) proved to be a masterstroke. Because once Drake became famous and his sister Chloe mentioned in an interview that the actress Elizabeth Melville had once been married to her brother, Liz suddenly became inundated with offers for acting roles.

Some of the roles she was offered were minimal, some major. Some of them did nothing for her career, some of them did quite a lot. And once her ex had pulled his disappearing act, Liz was always in the news, with everyone wanting to know where she thought he was hiding.

Of course that hullabaloo had died down after a while; but now, with Drake's proposed reappearance from whatever dark cavern he'd been hibernating in, and with a new novel to sell, the media were certain to remember her again, sparking even more acting roles, and hopefully some interest from Hollywood.

And then came yesterday morning.

***

Yesterday, Liz awoke to a very strange feeling. A bad feeling, that was. After getting out of bed, she'd walked opposite into Frankie's bedroom to make sure that he was all right. She didn't know why, but her worries all revolved around her son.

Frankie wasn't in his room, which at first worried Liz even more, until she finally found him in the living room of their apartment.

But this was where things began to get creepy.

Frankie had been watching television, the early morning cartoons as usual, but on hearing her behind him, he got up and turned to face her.

All at once Liz had realized that something was wrong. Her autistic son's face, normally so deadpan and with a liquid thread of drool running from either the left or right corner of his mouth, now seemed normal.

Indeed, Frankie himself now appeared to have been miraculously cured of his inexplicable mental issues.

Liz had no time however to consider this miracle cure in detail, because Frankie, who hadn't spoken a single legible word in years, now began speaking in perfect English.

"Hi, mom, dad has a message for you. He says to tell you to come along with Auntie Melody, to come see him in Raynham in Massachusetts tomorrow. Auntie Melody knows the way and she'll be contacting you shortly with the details of your trip there."

Liz just gaped at him, and he went on speaking in his little boy's voice, which somehow sounded more grownup than it should have, an impression made even stronger and stranger by the fact that little Frankie Melville was the spitting image of his father: blonde hair, brown eyes and everything else.

"And, mom," Frankie went on, "dad is very serious about this. Make sure you go to Raynham with Auntie Melody tomorrow."

"Should I bring you along too?" Liz asked, confused, but seeing no other option than to go along with the crazy flow.

Her son slowly shook his head. "No, you're to leave me with granddad." And then, before Liz could ask the obvious next question, Frankie added: "Mrs. Bergman won't be coming in tomorrow: she's going to fall very ill this evening. That's what dad says."

The young boy smiled at Liz again, almost melting her heart with how normal he now looked.

And then, just like that, it was all over. Normalcy drained out of him like air escaping a punctured balloon. It was horrifying, seeing his intellect deflate like this, like watching a normal person become a flesh and blood puppet. Frankie's previously animated face went slack again, and he seemed to slip back into the clutches of idiocy. Spaghetti-thick strings of drool spurted from both corners of his mouth and messed up his blue Donald Duck pajamas.

Liz bust into tears at the horrible sight.

Ignoring her, Frankie turned back to watch Bugs Bunny again.

Liz was still crying, tears streaming down her cheeks, when her cellphone rang. On walking back into her bedroom and picking it up, she was shocked to see the caller: Melody Melville. The woman had never called her before.

Liz was even more stunned to hear *why* Melody was calling her.

"Hey, just hear me out," Melody said in her breathless honey-toned voice. "I won't blame you if you think I'm crazy. But I just got this text message from Drake, asking me and you to come and see him in Raynham tomorrow."

"No, I don't think you're crazy!" Liz managed to blurt out. "Drake just contacted me too." She frowned at her open bedroom door, at the cartoon sounds coming from the living room, and shivered again. "Honey, you don't wanna know *how* he told me. I'm still creeped out just thinking about it."

Talking to Melody had been therapeutic, making her feel better, confirming to her that no, she wasn't crazy; that no, she wasn't losing her mind; that yes, her 5-year-old autistic son *had* just spoken to her and given her instructions that were supposedly from his missing father.

"Hey, I think we need to get together on this," Melody said. "We need to plan. Is it alright if I drive over to your place right now?"

Liz almost said no. She could hear the other woman's happy anticipation in her voice, and it made her jealous that someone else could be so happy when she was at the moment so sad and depressed. But she put the bad feeling aside and nodded into the phone.

"Sure, come on over," she replied. "It's Friday, but I'm not filming this weekend." At the moment Liz had a good role in Soap City, a soap opera about—of all things—the travails of getting a soap opera made. Liz played the part of a hassled female executive who was trying to juggle work and motherhood after her jealous and faithless husband had left her for a less-employed woman.

"Thanks," Melody said, "expect me in about an hour."

Liz nodded at the phone again. The old house where she and Drake had lived while they were married, and which he'd retained the mortgage to even though he was now a wealthy man, was on the northwest side of Dayton. Considering that Melody had sounded like she was in a hurry, Liz figured one hour was just enough time for the woman to have her bath, eat a bite of breakfast and then drive northeast, over here to the Village at Cloud Park Apartments where Liz resided.

In the meantime, while awaiting Melody's arrival, Liz had busied herself with her own preparations. Now that Melody had phoned her, she put out of her mind any thoughts of not responding to Drake's invitation.

Oh, I'm definitely going to Raynham to see him, and not just because he's asking me to come.

Because it had now occurred to Liz for the first time, that Drake was either somehow responsible for Frankie's mentally deficient condition or might hold the cure to it.

And like every good mother, she was prepared to do whatever it took to get her child well again.

Melody had arrived on schedule an hour later, with her bags already packed and ready to spend the night with Liz . . . And the rest was their drive over here with Bonnie in tow.

***

When Liz arrived back at the dinner table, Seer Jonah was discussing the sleeping arrangements for that night.

"The house has three bedrooms," he explained. "Two upstairs and one downstairs. The way I figure it, the two misses Melvilles, Melody and Liz, will both share the master bedroom." He punctuated his comment with a smile. "This is after all their husband's house."

"Hey, I'm divorced from Drake," Liz reminded him. "I've even got the alimony to prove it."

That statement got the men in the room laughing.

Seer Jonah laughed too at her curt reply. "Is anyone ever truly divorced from their feelings?" he then asked in a soft voice.

His question caught Liz unawares. She realized she had no answer for it. She glanced sideways at Melody, to see how she was interpreting Jonah's question. *Oh dammit, the last thing I need now is for her to think I'm here to steal her husband. If she thinks I'm trying to get Drake back it's going to be a long trip.*

But no, Melody still seemed cool and unoffended, and while Liz watched her for an adverse reaction, the transsexual woman's lips shaped themselves into a smile.

When Liz made no further reply, Seer Jonah looked around at the rest of them. "Todd and Nick will share the other upstairs bedroom, which is actually my room, while Chloe and Bonnie will take the large guest room downstairs."

"But where will you sleep then?" Bonnie asked, though Liz noticed that she seemed both delighted and distressed by the sleeping arrangements.

Upset because it means I won't be in the same bed as her, Liz thought absently, *but also relieved because these pairings mean she'll have female protection from Seer Jonah, who seems stuck on her.*

"Oh, I'll be fine down here on the living room couch," the tattooed man replied Bonnie. "It's just for a night anyway."

CHAPTER 4

The Bleeding Oysters: The BIG Fuss!

Drake Melville's novel *The Bleeding Oysters* was a runaway international bestseller, one that to date had sold over 25 million copies worldwide.

But the book had created great controversy.

The Bleeding Oysters was a compendium of the most lewd, perverted and disgusting acts known to man, both in the sexual arena and elsewhere. Needless to say, the book was almost universally panned by critics, which of course only helped both its notoriety and sales.

Every generation needs its own Marquis de Sade it seems, and for the Facebook, Twitter, YouTube and Instagram generation Drake Melville admirably fulfilled this purpose, this function of spitting in the face of everything society considered decent, commendable and worthy of emulation.

It was generally agreed by all and sundry that Drake Melville's epic tale (the book *The Bleeding Oysters* being 1000-plus pages long) of its hero Seer Jonah's actions while seeking personal enlightenment and sexual satisfaction, had no redeeming qualities whatsoever.

Indeed, even the most jaded literary palate must needs admit that this strung-together tale of ceaseless rape, torture and mutilation, child and animal abuse (including both child and animal rape and mutilation), sadism and masochism, penultimate blasphemy, unspeakably horrific magic rituals, gore and sleaze (and gory sleaze) urolagnia and coprophagy, imbibing of one's own semen as an elixir, and forced self-cannibalism and mass necrophilia should never have seen the light of day in a bookshop, or even up on the virtual bookshelves of Amazon.com.

As Amber Hauptmann of the Literary Hedonist Book Review scathingly wrote: "In *The Bleeding Oysters*, it's as if the Devil himself has found a prophet in Mr. Melville. Apparently the Devil has a lot to say to mankind and Drake Melville says it admirably well. This is not in any way to approve of this nonsensical excuse for so-called literature, but rather to marvel at the seeming lack of any limits of obscenity and depravity that untalented hack writers such as Drake Melville are willing to sink to in order to make a quick buck. It also makes one wonder if Mr. Melville's publisher Chaos House is secretly run by a coven of witches who are doing their best to herald the coming of the Antichrist."

In the novel, Seer Jonah was a resident of a strange and distorted realm called the Static Earth, a fictional duplicate of the known world, but one which had stopped spinning on its axis, so that half of it lay permanently in daytime and half permanently in night, with both realms separated by an equally permanent zone of twilight.

Like many religious leaders, Seer Jonah believed that the way to God was through personal suffering.

However, his own beliefs differed in one major aspect from established religious doctrine, which was this: if you were too weak or lacked the required self-discipline to suffer by your own hand, Seer Jonah was willing to help you suffer, to put you through so much agony in fact, that God Almighty would pity you and automatically pardon your sins; so that in the event of your horrible and pathetic death, which was certain to come at Jonah's own hands when he was done with mutilating, raping, torturing and occasionally eating selected choice parts of you, when this was all accomplished, God Almighty would then feel obliged to admit you into whichever paradise you professed faith in.

(This fictional man was just morally reprehensible, well deserving of his infamy and the title of 'Most Evil Man Who Ever Lived.' Take for instance, the book's 'Necrosy' chapter, in which, to summon a demigod, Jonah had unearthed the corpses of a mother and her newborn baby who had both recently died in a car accident. To perform the ghastly ritual, Seer Jonah had cut the dead woman open, reinserted the baby into her womb and stitched her up again, and then copulated with her corpse six times; after which he'd extracted the rotting infant from its dead mother's belly again and roasted it to feed the beast-creature he'd called up from Hell's abyss.)

This then was Seer Jonah's evil doctrine, and one which he practiced with great passion and dedication all through the pages of *The Bleeding Oysters*.

The book's title was a reference to the equally infamous Scandinavian sorcerer Ola Mimi whose favorite breakfast had been the sliced-in-half testicles of young boys eaten raw, hence the term 'bleeding oysters.'

Of course good people everywhere didn't take this nonsense (or literary ass-fucking) lying down. The book was vilified worldwide and was even the subject of mass public burnings, though its now-famous author merely laughed at this show of public disdain and thanked those who'd burnt his book for buying it in the first place.

Book signings were picketed by adults concerned for the safety of their bodily orifices, parents concerned for their children, pet owners concerned for their animals, and even bereaved people concerned for their corpses; this last category being worried because Seer Jonah had claimed in the novel that a dead and rotting human vagina, anus, or mouth provided much sweeter sexual pleasures than that of a living dog, cat, or goat, which in turn provided greater pleasures than a normal male or female body.

Seer Jonah also claimed that puppy and kitten fat made the best sexual lubricant of all, this fat being best extracted by boiling the freshly-killed bodies of said puppies and kittens. Pet skin also supposedly made great footwear and underwear.

Even goldfish owners weren't left out of the animal rights protests, with Drake (via Jonah of course) claiming that sticking four or five live goldfish (or a pair or trio of axolotls) up a woman's vagina during her monthly period would give her the most enjoyable of orgasms.

And so, scandalized thousands protested and called for the book to be banned.

But of course, no one paid any attention to these sane voices of protest. After all, Drake's novel was selling like hot cakes, with ten million copies already bought by the time the hullabaloo was reaching this crescendo. And so the age-old excuse was given to keep it in publication, which was, that extreme and over-the-top art had no true lasting negative effects on the public consciousness, and that those miscreants who put into practice things they read about in books already had those evil thoughts and intents in their psychotic and weak minds.

This argument, which had already proved extremely successful in defusing criticism of overly violent or overly sexualized Hollywood films, once again worked its illogical magic, and soon no one dared criticize Drake's 'morbid masterpiece' as *The Bleeding Oysters* was now being called, particularly once Drake publicly proved himself to be LGBT friendly by marrying the very pretty Melody Kaye.

The book kept selling and Drake and Melody Melville were a very rich and very happy high-profile celebrity couple much sought after for parties and interviews.

And then the really strange thing happened:

One bright summer morning three years ago, a distraught and tearful Melody Melville announced to the American public that her beloved husband was missing.

At first everyone assumed this to be just a publicity stunt. But Drake's vanishing was soon confirmed to be true. An extensive and expensive search by several private investigators turned up nothing, as the missing author had predicted in the letters he'd left for his wife, literary agent, publishers, and solicitors.

Of course this renewed notoriety merely increased the sales of his bestseller novel.

Drake's letters had said he'd 'left town' for 'Parts Unknown' to work on his new novel, tentatively titled *The Book of Atrocities*; a novel that he claimed would completely eclipse *The Bleeding Oysters* in every possible aspect, and one that would revolutionize the literary scene forever.

While these two possibilities did leave Drake's legions of fans and detractors salivating from the thought of future opportunities to praise and criticize him, the question persisted: where was he?

Yes, exactly where had Drake Melville vanished to?

CHAPTER 5

Chloe

When dinner was over, the six guests broke up into three groups to attend to assigned tasks. Nick and Todd went to get their gear from their car, as did Liz and Melody. This left Chloe and Bonnie to assist Seer Jonah in clearing the dinner table and doing the dishes.

Chloe decided to use this opportunity to once more query Jonah, seeing as he'd not given her a reply when she'd asked during dinner.

"So, where *is* Drake hiding out?" she asked now, while scraping congealed spaghetti off of a plate into the trash can. Bonnie meanwhile, was loading up the dishwasher.

Chloe first thought that the man wouldn't reply her. But finally he broke his silence, looked up from wiping down the kitchen counter, and smiled at her.

"Oh, your brother is somewhere across town," he said in an infuriating cool voice that made her think he was taunting her.

"And it's so secret that you couldn't take us directly there? Hey, man, gimme a break. I'm his *blood* sister, for crying out loud. Drake and I have been together since childhood and we love each other. So give me a hint, please, as to why he's doing this?"

Bonnie looked up from putting more plates into the dishwasher and nodded, a half-smoked cigarette dangling from the left corner of her mouth. Chloe noted that since Seer Jonah had announced that she and Bonnie would be rooming together Bonnie seemed more upbeat. But then too, the tall and thin woman also had an air of resigned disappointment to her, as if a great desire and expectation of hers had been thwarted.

Hey, you can't win 'em all, sister, she thought on remembering what Nick had said about Bonnie's sapphic desire for Liz.

"Yeah, I'm curious too," Bonnie said. "This all seems so cloak-and-dagger to me. It's like Drake is scared that someone's after him. In fact, that's the interpretation of his vanishing that I always give Liz—that he's hiding from someone who is out to murder him."

Chloe nodded her agreement with Bonnie. "Yes, that makes worrying sense. I've been thinking along those lines too for a long time. Considering the content of his novel *The Bleeding Oysters,* it's no far stretch of the imagination to assume Drake had gotten death threats from some right-wing group, either political or religious."

Bonnie puffed out smoke. "But according to Liz, you never mentioned any such thing to her."

"Oh, Liz wouldn't know. She and Drake have hardly been in contact since breaking up . . . I actually find it rather weird that he's asking for her now? Yeah, so if Drake was gonna discuss his fears with anyone, it's either me or Melody he'd have told. But he never told me anything. And I speak to Melody regularly and she's never suggested any such thing either." Chloe passed the scraped plates to Bonnie and paused for a moment, leaning against the kitchen counter with a frown on her face. "Nor, for that matter, did Drake ever indicate any such worries about assassination in those texts of his which Melody showed me."

Still very perplexed, she looked at Seer Jonah again. "Which brings us back to square one. I . . . we . . . still have no idea why at the height of his fame, my elder brother suddenly packed up his bags and left for *Parts Unknown.*" She jabbed her finger into Jonah's chest. "And you, mystery man, have all the answers, but aren't telling."

Seer Jonah laughed. "You're very impatient, you know. If you've waited for years to see him, what difference does a single additional night make?"

He turned away from her and began lathering up the chopping board in the sink.

"When you put it like that, you make it sound so simple," Bonnie said, finally shutting the dishwasher and turning it on. "Hey, I need a fresh cigarette," she added, then walked out from the kitchen to the dining room to get herself one.

"It is simple," Seer Jonah told Chloe after Bonnie had left. "As the whole world knows, your brother went into seclusion to work on his new book. And now he's finished it. You're a journalist. You must know that writers do this all the time—shut themselves away in some lonely retreat so that they can concentrate better."

Chloe searched for a reply to this that would bait him into revealing the truth. But she was unable to come up with any. She felt that he'd defeated her; which upset her because, as a reporter she was used to ferreting out the truth. And in this case, she suspected that there was a lot more to her brother's abrupt and shocking disappearance three years ago than merely his intense desire to write in peace.

She nodded at Seer Jonah. "You win, man. We'll all find out tomorrow then."

Bonnie reentered the kitchen with a fresh cigarette stuck between her lips. She was also carrying the empty wine bottles from their dinner.

"Alright," she announced, "the others have left our bags in the living room for us to pick up when we're ready."

Seer Jonah smiled at her and then turned away to clean the meat cleavers in the sink. He raised one of the broad-bladed knives and examined its glossy surface with intense concentration.

And it was then, triggered by the combination of the man's crazy tattoos, his rapt facial expression as he ran his thin fingers along the cleaver's sharp edge, and the size of the blade itself, that Chloe had a sudden damning feeling of terror.

For a seemingly timeless interlude, while Bonnie set the empty wine bottles down on the kitchen counter and departed with a tray to fetch the wineglasses, Chloe collapsed against the edge of the kitchen counter and gripped it tightly to prevent herself from slipping to the floor in a faint.

Seer Jonah was still studying his meat cleaver. He was facing away from her, and was unaware of her distress; she was looking at the spiral of crimson writing that ascended from the back of his neck to the top of his head.

Since Chloe didn't understand the language they were written in, 'obscene and blasphemous' were strange terms to describe Seer Jonah's inkings; but that was the impression that came to her: that that indecipherable script told of nauseating rites and atrocious magical deeds so horrible that they would give her endless nightmares if she could interpret the red writing.

As if hypnotized to look, her gaze crept around the side of the tattooed man's head until she caught the reflection of his face in the flat surface of the brightly polished blade he was studying.

She flung her hand to her mouth to choke off her gasp of horror.

What she saw reflected in the blade wasn't a human face, but rather a puddle of swirling darkness, in which human features were mocked by black pits and slashes in dripping tar. She looked back at Seer Jonah, wondering if his head had begun melting, but no, he was still completely normal. And yet, when Chloe peered again at his reflection in the cleaver blade, the same distortions had once more been introduced to his face; it was no face at all, just evil chaos mocking true order. And this was no trick of the light either, the man's tattooed neck appeared normal enough in the damning reflection.

It was horrifying to look at, making Chloe shiver and gasp for breath; and yet its unpleasantness and strangeness were the least of the terrors it created in her. Overwhelming everything else, and almost causing Chloe Melville to swoon like a princess who on her wedding night discovers she's married a frog and not the prince, was the fact that she suddenly understood the words tattooed on Seer Jonah's head. And if anything, their meaning was much worse than she'd suspected, speaking of deeds of evil that far eclipsed anything her mind could conceive of. She still didn't understand the language, but, triggered by the man's hideous transformation in the mirror of the cleaver blade, a translation came to her mind, as if the mirror-monster were speaking telepathically to her. Also, the words on Jonah's body seemed to have come alive, wriggling like red worms over his skin.

She began gasping with fright, wanting to flee from the kitchen, but too enervated by fear to give action to this heartfelt desire. So she stood there, with the words' nauseating meanings raging through her soul like a psychic chainsaw slicing up her sanity.

Then she felt someone shaking her.

"Are you alright?" Bonnie was asking her.

Chloe jerked her eyes open. She was still leaning against the kitchen counter.

Huh? When did I shut my eyes?

Seer Jonah was still washing at the sink, but now he'd put down the cleaver and was scrubbing a meat skewer clean while humming to himself. Chloe stared at him for a long moment, while Bonnie stared at her in turn, wondering what the matter was.

"Hey, you okay?" Bonnie asked again, blowing smoke right in her face.

Chloe, who didn't smoke, coughed and sputtered as the cigarette smoke went down her airways. "Help me out of here," she whispered to Bonnie. "I think I had too much to drink with dinner."

Seer Jonah turned at their conversation. "Are you okay?" he asked Chloe.

Before replying, she stared at him for a long moment. The meaning of his tattoos had fled her mind the moment she opened her eyes, and she no longer remembered any of the deeds they recorded, but the dread of him which they had summoned still held her firmly in its grip. Though Seer Jonah now looked ordinary (innocent? benign? harmless?) again, she now 'knew'—though it was of course impossible—that this man standing with she and Bonnie wasn't truly human.

"I'm fine," she finally replied him with a quick nod. "But I think I'll go to bed now."

She looked back at him as Bonnie helped her out of the kitchen. He was staring after them with concern written on his face. But Chloe wasn't deceived in the least. She wished she could dredge up the memory of what those evil words on his body meant, and hold them concrete in her mind. But it was impossible; all their meaning had left her, just as surely as his alternate 'melted-tar-face' was no longer reflected in the cleaver blade now lying beneath the soapy surface of the water in the sink.

Bonnie steered her through the living room, past Nick and Todd who were watching a Super Bowl replay, and helped her to their room, which was very large and very clean, with a giant bed with floral sheets.

Then Bonnie left her in bed and went to help finish cleaning up.

"You just relax in here. I'll bring in our bags later," she said before leaving.

Chloe felt scared to see her go. But she realized that it would be wrong to ask her to stay. For one thing it would be impolite to their host. For another, she'd already begun feeling silly about her own fears.

So instead, she told Bonnie: "Hey, when you're coming in to sleep, help me fetch my cellphone too. I think I left it on the kitchen counter."

"Will do," Bonnie said and shut the door.

No, I'm not gonna give in to fear, Chloe decided as she lay alone in the bed, *I'm gonna get a grip on myself.*

She was a reporter and a tough young woman.

Hell, she told herself, *maybe I'm not as tough as Todd, who was a both a marine and a war correspondent, but I'm definitely tougher than Nick, who pukes each time we view a stiff in the morgue. Alright, I know what I saw back there in the kitchen. But did I really see it? The way his face changed like that; it could have been merely a trick of the light. Dammit, I'll never know. And I can't tell the others, they'll just assume I'm crazy. But Seer Jonah? Seer Jonah? Oh shit! Not human? Of course the creepy sonofabitch is human! All this is just the power of suggestion working on me. Like everyone else I read Drake's crazy book, and now I'm meeting a person who looks like the book's main character, but no . . . no, no, no, I'm not gonna let it get to me. A reflection speaking telepathically to me? That's padded cell stuff! Hell no, I'm not letting my imagination run away. No, I'm not about cracking up here. Not tonight, when the big day is tomorrow.*

She grinned. *Eat your hearts out and die of envy, newbitches! I'm the one who'll be breaking the news that we found Drake Melville! Hahaha!*

As she lay there in bed staring at the ceiling, she heard Liz and Melody talking outside the house; it sounded like they were on the front porch.

A cool breeze blew in through the open window. Chloe felt there was something unpleasant about the breeze.

For a moment she felt a return of her fears. She felt a strong compulsion to charge outside and try to convince the others to leave this house tonight.

Then she gave up in resignation. *But I can't leave. This is my big break as a journalist.* Writhing in frustration, she beat her palms against the bed sheets. *Damn it. Damn it! Now, I've got a real bad feeling about tomorrow and yet I've gotta see it through, no matter what! Hey, Drake, when I see you tomorrow you'd better have a really good explanation for putting me through this!*

A short while later she fell soundly asleep.

CHAPTER 6

Liz

It was almost nine-thirty before Liz glanced at her watch. "Oh my God, how time flies when you're having fun," she joked with Melody.

Melody giggled. "Yeah, you're right," she agreed. "I don't know if it's the fact that I'm delighted that tomorrow I'm finally going to see Drake again after all this while, or all the wine we had with dinner, but I haven't laughed like this in a long, long time. At the moment I feel so refreshed, so free, so ecstatic. It's a glorious feeling."

Liz knew what she meant. She felt similarly, as if tomorrow—oh, how few hours away, only a single night to get through now—would mark a definite turning point in her life.

She was however careful not to let Melody see how she felt. Now that there was a rapport between them, no matter how tenuous, she didn't want to do anything to damage their fledgling connection. It was always better to have friends than enemies, even if the friend was your ex-husband's new wife.

Anyway, Liz had found Melody to be a bag of surprises. The woman was funny, cultured, and very intelligent; not to mention disarmingly pretty. Wondering if this was how she herself had seemed to Bonnie earlier, she nonetheless could not resist sneaking glances at her companion while they sat side-by-side on the steps of the darkened front porch with the lambent moon glowing down on them both, imbuing the air with a sense of unspoken romantic possibilities.

Yes, although she'd tried to fight it all the while they'd been sitting here next to one another, Liz had felt the return of her earlier erotic stirrings. Her crotch felt hot, her nipples felt like sweating beads glued to her chest. The feeling wasn't a constant one, however, but one that came and went, ebbing and flowing like the tides, as if it too were controlled by the moon above.

What on earth is the matter with me? she wondered to herself; enjoying the feeling but too nervous to do anything about it. *Why is this woman making me so horny?*

Though a cooling breeze blew occasionally, the weather was now warmer than it had been when they'd arrived in Raynham. Both women still wore their jeans and tee shirts, and Liz admired the smooth curve of Melody's breasts through her top.

Occasionally they'd hear loud male noises from inside the house; a cheer or a groan. That was Nick and Todd watching the replay of last year's Super Bowl and either applauding a touchdown or cussing a lost opportunity.

So far Liz and Melody had had a very funny conversation. Melody had been an actress too before Drake had married her, but she'd not been a successful one, and some of the stories she told Liz about her failed attempts to garner recognition in the film industry filled Liz with empathy for her.

Other stories had Liz in stitches, like the one where Melody had gone drunk to an audition where she was supposed to act the part of a drunken woman and nobody had noticed the difference.

"It was just crazy," Melody said, trying to hold her laughter in so as not to either disturb their friends in the house or alarm anyone walking past the foot of the driveway. "Really, I mean it. Alright, see, so here I was, so sloshed that I could barely stand on my two feet and the director keeps telling me how great a performance I was putting on. Of course I got the part."

And then she sighed with regret. "That damn movie would have been my big break too, except that the director had a fight with the sponsors over something or other—I think it was the amount of nudity desired in the film: the director wanted more, the sponsors wanted less—and in the end they cut the funding for it."

Liz didn't say anything. She too was familiar with movie projects losing funding. The same thing had happened to her several times before she'd begun getting noticed.

Finally though, the weather turned a little cold again and both women got to their feet.

"Well, I guess it's time to turn in," Melody said, and they entered the house together. They'd already taken their luggage upstairs, so now it was merely a question of waving goodnight to Nick and Todd, and ascending the stairs with Melody in the lead.

Both men however seemed so deeply engrossed in their sports program that Liz doubted they'd even heard the pair of spoken 'goodnights,' though Todd did wave reluctantly at them as if shooing them from the living room. He and Nick had grim looks on their faces as they watched the burly men onscreen race up and down the gridiron like they were demon-possessed.

"Men," Melody smirked in amusement as they climbed the stairs. "It's like the world's gonna end if their team's losing."

Liz yawned. Now that she felt sleepy she also felt less aroused, which she was grateful for. Melody had so far shown no signs of being either similarly turned on or at least equally attracted to her, and so this lessening of her own sexual desire was a clear blessing in her favor, seeing as it helped to prevent an awkward situation from developing between them, which might prove to be particularly embarrassing as they would be sharing the same bed tonight.

Though dammit, some sex tonight would be nice, she thought. *It'll help me sleep better and also take my mind off tomorrow.*

But she wasn't a slut, banging men she hardly knew on a moment's notice to scratch her genital itches; and also, the pickings here were anorexic-catwalk-model slim. She didn't fancy Nick, and Todd, who she did like, was happily married; and Liz didn't consider herself to be any kind of a home wrecker.

"Don't you think it's strange that we're all being crammed into three rooms?" Liz asked Melody as they climbed. "Is it really true that this building only has three bedrooms? Judging from the size of the house, I'd have thought there'd be at least one or two more."

Melody nodded. "I know what you mean. There actually should be more rooms upstairs, but there's a balcony at the back of the house that looks out over the rear yard and into the surrounding countryside. It's an odd construction, long and wide, and it totally splits the roof into two halves at the back. I'll admit that the view from there is spectacular however."

She grinned at Liz then and tugged on her arm. "Hey, you know what—let's go out onto the balcony and look around."

Liz shook her head. "Nah, not tonight. I'm bushed. Maybe in the morning before we drive across town to see Drake."

Melody shook her head as they both stepped up onto the upper landing. "Oh, come on, don't be like that. Let's just step outside for a few minutes, just for a quick peek, so you'll see what it looks like and how nice the view is even at night. It really is a wonderful perspective."

With an invitation like that Liz felt it would be impolite to refuse, particularly since they'd been getting along famously so far.

"All right," she grudgingly agreed. "But only for a few minutes. I really need to get into bed."

***

The roof extension was semicircular and was covered by a dome like a garden pavilion, a marble concavity suspended over their heads by a ring of sturdy pillars. The forward end of the balcony, which looked out over the countryside, was cordoned off by a metal railing. There was no light out here. Melody had flicked the switch in the hallway before they stepped outside, but it hadn't worked. "The fixture must be broken," she'd said. "Either that or the bulb burnt out and Jonah didn't bother replacing it because he hardly comes out here at night."

"Now this is definitely unusual," Liz said as they stepped out over the concrete floor, which, the farther out they walked, felt abnormal beneath her feet. In fact the floor felt so unusual that finally she looked down at it to see why her feet kept slipping, and on noting the deep grooves in its otherwise smooth surface, turned on her cellphone flashlight and shone it on the ground.

"Oh that," Melody said on noticing her interest. "That was there when we bought the house. It has something to do with magic, I think. You know how interested in the supernatural Drake is."

Liz nodded slowly and then, being careful to keep her composure, she walked out of the area of the balcony where the strange markings were, turned back to face them, and then shone her light on them to see clearly what had been engraved into the concrete floor.

She gasped. There, in the middle of that semicircular enclosure, was a large pentagram.

"Uh-uh-uh," she stuttered as fear once more gripped her.

Her obvious state of shock and discomfort caused Melody to step out of the pentagram to join her.

"Oh, I'm sorry," Melody instantly apologized. "I didn't know it would upset you so much to see that. I'd forgotten it was there. I've actually only been here once since we bought the house. I saw no point to coming to Raynham anyway. It's just a little town with nothing to see and one that has a creepy reputation around these parts." She gave Liz a slight giggle and then flung an arm around her shoulders to comfort her. "And besides, our house in Long Beach is much nicer anyway."

"No, I'm okay," Liz said. "It's just so unexpected to see something like this in such an ordinary home. Hey, do you know who owned this house before you?"

Melody shrugged, then she turned Liz around so that she wasn't facing the pentagram anymore with its suggestion of evil rites. She steered her outward towards the metal railing, until they were both standing beside it and staring down at the backyard, which like the front yard had lots of trees; fruit trees from the smell of them. From this height the trees looked like giant green toadstools.

"Oh, I don't know," Melody finally replied the question. "The building was empty for quite a while before we bought it." She now seemed to have forgotten her previous reason for bringing her companion out here, that of showing her the view from the balcony. And for her own part, Liz was now so stunned and submerged in gloom by the sight of that huge pentagram on the floor, that she wouldn't have been able to appreciate even the Mona Lisa had a giant reproduction of it been hanging in the air above the house.

Then Melody tapped herself on the forehead. "Hey, I do remember now: Drake once told me that back in the fifties this place belonged to a witch, a woman named Erin de Mornay. Apparently she was quite famous or rather infamous in these parts, and across the USA in general. She was believed to have bewitched several people in the neighborhood to death. But of course that's just bullshit, the sort of superstitious crap that folks living in a small town will say to implicate an outsider."

Melody clearly didn't see the effect that her words had on her companion.

Famous or infamous? Liz shuddered to the core of her being. *Oh, how much like Drake that sounds.*

She still couldn't get her mind around the fact that the man she'd once loved had gone from writing innocent detective and thriller novels to penning something as over-the-top and nauseating as *The Bleeding Oysters*. While married to Drake, she'd read everything he'd written, and on later reading *The Bleeding Oysters* had been stunned: his famous novel seemed to her to have been written by a completely different person, one with no morals or scruples whatsoever.

Sacrifice! She remembered the pentagram behind her and that terrifying word howled in her mind like a banshee: *Sacrifice! Drake wants to sacrifice you here!* The very idea of such being the case was so farfetched however that she immediately dismissed the thought as silly.

She snapped out of her gloomy thoughts when she felt Melody's warm body pressing against hers. At first she attached no significance to this close contact; the weather was cool now and the feeling of one body touching another was a source of warmth for both of them.

But then she became aware of Melody's warm breath on her neck, and a few seconds later, of the touch of the other woman's lips against her left ear. Then to erase any doubts in her mind, Melody began gently nibbling on her ear.

Although confused and still in some shock from realizing that this house had a magical connection to the past that might already be endangering everyone now inside it, she managed to giggle and turn around to face Melody, all thoughts of admiring the view from up here now gone from her mind also.

"Oh, what are you doing?" she asked coyly, delighted that her concealed desire for the other woman was being reciprocated. This was totally unexpected though, as so far today Melody hadn't shown the slightest romantic interest in her.

"I'm just giving you what you want," Melody replied in a soft voice that sent erotic shivers down Liz's spine. Her fingers had meanwhile shifted to caressing Liz's shoulders, and then she wrapped her arms around her and pulled her close.

She leaned forward and kissed Liz, and Liz kissed her back hungrily, while wondering at these unusual actions of hers. The one time that she'd ever kissed a girl before this was in high school, a dare on her fifteenth birthday. And now? It was a heady feeling like she was growing intoxicated with alcohol. Despite which she tried to control herself, to keep cool amidst the burning between her thighs.

She slipped a hand between Melody's legs, felt the hardness there and squeezed it gently, making Melody tremble all over.

"Oh wow!" Melody gasped. "I've gotta have you right now, honey!"

Liz reluctantly pushed Melody away. "No, not out here," she said. "Someone will look out and see us."

This was true. The pavilion was open on both sides, clearly visible from both the master bedroom and from Seer Jonah's bedroom, where the guys would be rooming tonight. In fact, if they'd already left the living room, Nick and Todd might be spying on she and Melody right now. And then what a juicy and scandalous tale they'd have for Chloe, who was certain to pass it on to her brother. Liz winced at the thought of the emotional fireworks that such a disclosure might result in.

Thankfully, Melody shared her caution. "Yeah, you're right," she agreed, giving Liz's breasts a firm squeeze. "Let's go inside."

They made their way inside and hurried to their bedroom, where they both quickly undressed and leapt into the huge bed. Liz hadn't felt this aroused in a long time. By the time Melody went down on her, spreading her legs like a wishbone, she was as wet as a stream.

Squirming with pleasure and desiring to return the favor, she tapped the transsexual woman on her shoulder. "Let's sixty-nine!" she gasped.

Once Melody had turned around, she took the woman's short and fat penis in her mouth and began sucking. The result of this was unexpected: Melody instantly ejaculated in her mouth. Liz was too tied up in her own pleasure to spit out the come like she normally would. She swallowed it all down and was grateful that after Melody's orgasmic trembling had subsided, she instantly resumed her attentions on her clitoris. Melody's orgasm had primed Liz; a few more licks of tongue and she came too, letting out her breath in a long sustained gasp; it felt like her body was melting upwards and becoming moonlight.

"It's hard to call this cheating on Drake," Melody said afterwards. "He's been gone for three fucking years now and I haven't gotten fucked in all that time. And I love being fucked."

"You've never cheated on him?"

"No, I love him too much." She giggled. "And besides, the whole world was watching my every move anyway."

"So how've you managed then? Me, I'd go nuts if I had to remain celibate for that long."

"I just jerk off from time to time. A fat vibrator in my ass substitutes nicely for Drake's cock." She leaned up on her elbow and ran her fingers across Liz's breasts. "This is only the second time I've ever had sex with a woman. The first time was a mess; I couldn't get hard at all. But something about *you* . . ." She paused and let her fingers stray up to Liz's lips, and then, after Liz kissed their tips, trail further up her face to stroke her black hair. "You know, maybe it's because we both love Drake."

She pointed across the room at the huge mirror on the wall, where they were both reflected, their flesh naked and sweaty on the white sheets. "Hey, don't we just make a cute couple now?"

Liz leaned up and kissed Melody. "Hey, I know what your attraction to me is—you just wanna pay Drake back for abandoning you, by screwing his ex-wife."

Melody shrugged and then she burst out laughing. "Yeah, maybe. Same goes for you too—in your case, you'd be paying Drake back by screwing his current wife." Then she got up onto her knees and Liz saw that her penis was hard and throbbing again. "Oh, whatever the reason, let's do it again. I really want you."

She bent over and kissed Liz deeply, licking her tongue and the insides of her mouth. Liz had the sudden impression that Melody was savoring the taste of her semen on her tongue. The concept felt so perverse to her that, from being drowsy and ready to nod off, she found herself instead yearning to make love again.

"Yes, let's do it," she agreed, pushing her transsexual lover off of her and spreading her legs, so the woman could access her secret places.

Melody looked down at her spread thighs for some seconds and then shook her head. "Honey, it's not gonna work like that," she said.

Liz felt both amused and intrigued. "Why not? And what are you talking about anyway?" While speaking, she roved her hand back and forth beneath Melody's erection, playing with her testicles, which were quite large.

Melody trembled with pleasure at her caresses. Then she explained, while seemingly trying not to ejaculate prematurely in Liz's hand: "I just mean that you're gonna have to get on top. I'm much more used to being penetrated than taking the opposite position. Tonight, baby, you'll be doing all the thrusting."

That made sense to Liz. They were both women after all—and, with the fairer sex, lying back and taking it had been in vogue ever since the apes came down from the trees. And truth be told, she liked being on top anyway.

"Now it's my turn to be the boss," she growled, and then upended Melody so she was laying flat on her back, gasping with delight and anticipation. Then, after they had kissed passionately for a while, she squatted over the woman's stiff penis and slid herself down on it.

CHAPTER 7

Bonnie

"Hey, guys, looks like it's time to get some shut-eye," Todd said after crushing out his last cigarette in the weird ashtray shaped like a human skull. He got to his feet and handed Bonnie the TV's remote control. The football game was now over.

Nick got to his feet too and yawned. "Yeah, dude, I'm tired myself. Time for bed." He smiled at Bonnie. "See ya in the morning."

"Sleep tight." She waved at both men as they left the living room to ascend the stairs. And then, when she was left alone with the receding sound of their ascending footsteps, she turned her full attention to the television and began channel surfing.

She found a cooking show, a lifestyle show, and a rerun of *Survivor,* but none of them held her attention for very long. Finally she crossed the living room to appropriate the brass skull ashtray for her own use. Then she muted the TV and just sat in the chair Todd had vacated, smoking and thinking.

Anguished emotions coursed through her, upsetting and unsettling her with their intensity. She felt confused. She had no idea what to do. All she knew was that she wanted Liz. Bonnie didn't know if she was fully in love with Liz yet, but she knew that she felt a longing for her that totally eclipsed any emotions she'd felt for another person recently.

Bonnie Pierson had been married twice. She had two children from her first marriage, both of whom lived with their father, a TV producer. Bonnie herself ran a casting agency, which was how she'd originally met Liz Melville. That had been seven years ago, and their friendship had developed from there.

Bonnie had recently decided that men were too complicated to love, and figured it was about time she tried a relationship with a woman. And her best friend seemed the best candidate for her to fall in love with.

Though Liz was currently single, Bonnie had had no idea how to propose to her that they start dating. So she'd been approaching the matter of their having a romantic and sexual relationship in a roundabout way, by hinting and suggesting intimate things to do together until it would seem entirely natural for them to wind up in bed together.

The problem was, the longer this went on, the more she fell in love with her bestie, and now it hurt her deeply to realize that the object of her affection had no idea of her love for her.

Knowing the feeling wasn't mutual was almost driving Bonnie crazy, both increasing and dampening her heart's and body's desire for Liz.

Bonnie stared at the TV screen desperately, trying to focus on the current program that her fingers had strayed to—a report about Jessica Fox, a rich young heiress who'd suddenly turned up again after being missing for a whole year, but with no memory of where she'd been or what she'd done in the interim—but she couldn't get Liz out of her mind. Erotic images of Liz and Melody tormented her. Oh, what were they doing now?

Different lovemaking scenarios came to her flustered mind, all of them making her feel like shit, as if she'd lost her entire self-worth by desiring her friend.

She considered streaming something from Netflix on her laptop to distract herself from her thoughts, but then realized she was already too distracted.

Finally Bonnie couldn't take it anymore. Her cigarette burnt down to the filter and burnt her fingers. Wincing, she dropped the smoking stub into the ghoulish ashtray, but felt too troubled to light another cigarette.

Instead, slipping off her shoes and leaving the TV on, she left the living room and climbed the steps to the first floor.

As she reached the upper landing it occurred to her that she was being silly and was merely setting herself up for more heartache. But she couldn't help herself. She had to see. She had to know what was going on in the house's master bedroom.

So she padded on quietly down the upper hallway, relying on intuition to guide her to the bedroom she sought.

After passing a slightly ajar door through which moonlight and cool air spilled into the house, she was suddenly face-to-face with their bedroom door.

Oh my God, I was right, she thought in dismay on hearing the gasping and moaning coming from behind the door.

Saddened and shaken to the core of her being, Bonnie was about to turn around and head back the way she'd come, when she realized that the door wasn't locked, the lovers having been too wrapped up in themselves in their hurry to get into bed to make sure that it clicked properly shut.

Slowly, taking care not to make the slightest noise, Bonnie pushed the door open. She opened it until she could see the bed clearly.

She gasped at the sight of Liz, her own darling Liz, writhing atop that transsexual bitch slut Melody.

She stood there, feeling more shitty with each passing second and with each successive ramming of Liz's vagina down on Melody's penis, their combined gasping and moaning and jiggling breasts making her feel faint.

Then Liz flung her head back and let out a strangled gasp. Responding to this, Melody dug her fingernails deeply into Liz's ass cheeks, seemed to thrust up into the other woman with all of her might, and shut her eyes and seemed to be crying.

And then it was over, Bonnie's emotional torture complete. The two women, the one with the penis and the one without, lay side by side on the bed, smiling at each other and stroking each other's faces with languid fingers.

Bonnie felt crushed and depleted by what she'd just witnessed, but something (was it perhaps a masochistic desire to torment herself further?) kept her glued in place and made it impossible for her to walk away and thus save herself from further humiliation.

Knowing that she was merely hurting herself by remaining at her spying position, she nonetheless stayed there by the door to eavesdrop on their conversation. They didn't disappoint her.

"It was even better this time," Melody said. "No wonder Drake gets off so much on filling my butthole with his cock."

"You've never fucked Drake in the ass before?"

Melody shook her head. "Never. But that's cool with me. Personally I prefer the sensation and feeling of being a woman in bed, the experience of being made love to by a man. I am a woman after all."

"Oh, you're a hell of a woman alright," Liz agreed with a soft giggle that made Bonnie want to shoot herself from sheer rage.

You're mine, all mine, she thought. *You're my bestie and yet you do this to me with this bitch that you're meeting today for like what—the third time?* She felt crazy, her bosom full of a desire to charge into the bedroom and grab Liz by the throat and strangle her to death.

But then Bonnie admitted her defeat and sagged against the wall and sadness filled her.

I'd better just go back downstairs, smoke a cigarette and go to bed.

But Melody was once again speaking and Bonnie couldn't help but listen:

"You know I almost got into porn," Melody said. "And there they'd have fucked my ass off for real."

"You did?" Liz asked with drowsy interest. "You were going to do porno films?"

Melody leaned up on an elbow and nodded her head vigorously. "For real. I always tell Drake that he saved me from a lifetime of ass gaping. Actually, that was why I was at the book signing the day I met Drake. A friend of mine named KY was going to be there and we'd arranged to meet there since I lived nearby."

"You're pulling my leg, right? KY? Like the sexual lube? That's actually somebody's name?"

"Yeah it is. Her actual name is Kendra Yang, and she's trans like me. She helps run Titaholics Anonymous; they're a company that focuses on filming busty women; maybe you've heard of 'em?"

Liz shook her head sleepily. "No, I never heard of them before. I'm not into porn. I dislike it and never watch it. So I know nothing at all about that area of the movie biz, except that all the male performers have foot-long schlongs."

Melody laughed at that. "Well, I'm not really into that scene either, but I was flat broke and I needed some work and KY suggested I make some movies with her. She said I have the looks for it and could film some shemale-on-female scenes for kink appeal." Giggling, she leaned over and kissed Liz full on the lips. "But then I met your ex and my adult film career was over before it ever began. Thank God for that."

"I've had a few offers myself," Liz admitted to her with a yawn. "Mostly from companies wanting to cash in on Drake's success. But even if the money was excellent, I don't think I could handle getting banged by lots of anonymous enormous guys. My bestie Bonnie even tried talking me into doing some softcore flicks with the new company her friend was setting up, but I had to turn it down. I don't want to get typecast into that kinda thing, 'cos then producers and directors get the idea that that's what you do, and then offers for other sorts of acting work won't come in anymore, so it screws your entire career up."

"Yeah, I know what you mean. Oh, so Bonnie wanted you to do softcore?"

Liz nodded, though now it was clearly taking her an effort to remain awake. "Yeah, baby. You and I, we've clearly got more in common than just a husband and your come in my pussy!"

"Hahaha!"

Bonnie turned away fuming, her desire and sadness now once more replaced by rage. *Yes, I did suggest that you make those movies, you silly ungrateful cow, but you were broke at the time*—This was right after Drake had gone missing and his financial managers were unsure what to do with his money—*and when you said no I lent you the funds you needed anyway.*

As she stalked away along the corridor Bonnie knew she was being unfair to Liz, but she felt too betrayed by the sexual encounter she'd witnessed to think otherwise.

And this was her state of mind when she once again reached the slightly ajar door through which a soft breeze was entering the house.

She would have walked past it this time too, except that now she noticed a soft sustained glow streaming in also, as if someone had lit a fire outside on the balcony.

Too angry to be cautious and desperately in need of a distraction to take her mind off its negative emotions, Bonnie pulled the door fully open and stepped outside onto the balcony.

She was surprised; very surprised. This place was unlike any balcony she had ever been on before. It was semicircular in shape and had a high domed roof suspended by carved stone pillars; and it was bordered by metal rails.

But what really caught and held Bonnie's attention on the balcony, was the man who was standing in the exact middle of the giant pentagram cut into the center of the marble floor, the man glowing with a soft orange light that clearly came from the lines of writing that covered his now completely naked body.

Bonnie noticed this and noticed also that Seer Jonah's penis was hard, and was pointing at her like a compass's pointer. His penis was also tattooed, with more of those glowing red lines spiraling around it to its tip.

She felt the erection was summoning her and so walked towards it, while Seer Jonah stretched out his arms as if to welcome her.

"I called you and you came," he said with a cold but pleased smile.

Bonnie had no idea what he was talking about—*Honey, I came up here for someone else entirely, definitely not to meet with you*—but seeing him naked like this, she instantly realized that here was her chance, her opportunity to both relieve herself of her sexual frustration and also get some payback (if only minor and only in her own mind) on the woman—no, the *two* women—who had betrayed her tonight.

Yes, she should have been alarmed at the way the writing on his body was glowing from his bald head to his feet; but strangely, this sight of Seer Jonah all lit up like a Christmas tree in August seemed entirely natural to her and she felt no fear of him. All of her earlier trepidation and suspicions of this man had now magically departed from her psyche.

And so, as he stretched out his hands towards her, Bonnie went to him willingly, her heart full of desire, her sex dripping wet, knowing that this man, this tattooed man whose tattoos were blazing like fire, was what she wanted now and possibly forevermore. She was unaware of taking off her clothes, but when she stepped into the pentagram and he took her in his muscular if thin arms, she realized she had gotten naked on the trip to him.

She wanted to kiss him, to love him with a fierce love, to transfer all of her heartfelt desire for Liz to him, but when she brought her lips up to his he pushed her gently away.

"No," he said, pushing her down onto her knees with a gentle but firm pressure on her shoulders. "Kiss my cock. That is what you really want. It is your true master and your true lover. Tonight I will save you and deliver you from yourself."

Once again Bonnie had no idea what he meant. However she did what he said and kneeling, took his stiff and glowing penis into her mouth.

The penis was warmer than normal but it didn't burn her, and as she sucked on it, she had the sensation, the feeling, that its glowing words were visible through the skin of her face. For a moment it occurred to her that she was bewitched, as was everyone else in the house. It also occurred to Bonnie that if *she* could see the glow coming from Seer Jonah's body, it should also be visible to those others in the building, as she'd now realized that this strange pavilion-like balcony was clearly visible from the pair of bedroom windows that flanked it.

But this was a minor concern to Bonnie. Sucking on Seer Jonah's hard penis filled her with an inexplicable ecstasy. He thrust himself deep between her lips and she grabbed his thighs to steady herself, his slim but study legs feeling like the pillars of the Earth to her delicate fingers. She felt him tremble a little as she fellated him, felt his strong fingers in her hair. And both his touch on her body and her touch on his glowing skin filled her with the deepest elation.

"Now get down on your hands and knees," he finally ordered, "and let me save you. Let me show you the light of deepest darkness."

He helped her down on all fours, with her face pointing outward at the railing and the yard, and then got behind her.

She came the moment he entered her. It was the most exquisite orgasm imaginable; the sort of overwhelming climax that one reads about in books on sex but thinks is fiction. He rode her hard, like an animal, but she couldn't get enough of him.

She felt his body tense as if he was going to come. She had already come several times by now and wanted to feel his love milk inside of her body, as a confirmation of his love for her and her submission to him. She was weak and trembling and willing for anything now. And so when, just before it felt like he was going to flood her with his semen, he pulled out instead, she thought he was going to enter her anus; and she was ready for it. She reached a hand back and spread her buttocks wide.

"Yes, come in my ass," she said, wanting him, really wanting him in her tight fecal hole, which now began spasming in anticipation of his entry.

But instead, he roughly shoved her forward, so that she lay gasping on her side in the middle of the pentagram, and then produced a knife, a glittering knife.

She gazed at her reflection in the clear and shiny blade, willing it to come much closer so that she could see her sweaty and ecstatic face better. The glowing words on her lover's arms hypnotized her, and so, even when she felt a sudden terror, she found herself (for the third time now) unable to do a thing about it.

"No!" she screamed. But even though she opened her mouth as wide as she could, till her lips felt like they were ripping apart at both ends, the words were vacuumed out of her throat and taken away somewhere else, to a terrible place where approving ears heard them and ungodly appetites fed on them; ears and hungers not belonging to those she wished to summon help from.

And then the blade met her flesh. Razor sharp, she felt it slice deeply into her neck with no hesitation in the thrust. She felt the agonizing bite of metal going in; she felt the liquid of her life pour out, warmly jetting out.

Intense pain, regret, and sorrow filled her. She felt darkness as a sentient entity, reaching out icy welcoming fingers and pulling her into itself; turning her soul into food, meat for creatures that were themselves fleshless.

"Now you journey to the darkness, "Seer Jonah said in an excited voice, standing up and masturbating over her, spraying his semen on her dying body, as it twitched on the carved marble floor like the body of a deer hit by a car. The semen spattered her and burnt like acid.

More betrayal, she thought in dismay. *I'm betrayed again—twice tonight by those I love!*

As Bonnie died, she watched her blood flow out along the deep grooves that made up the pentagram, meeting and connecting at the enclosed star's angles. And as her blood flowed, it too began glowing a bright orange like the words on Seer Jonah's body.

And now something was happening to the world around Bonnie. It seemed to be changing, as if the laws of reality were being rewritten as she watched.

Everything remained the same, but it was now different in some way.

"Die, bitch," Seer Jonah said as the light of life left Bonnie's open-and-staring eyes for good.

And Bonnie Pierson died, as ignorant as a lamb on a chopping block, not understanding in the least what had just happened to her, or what was going on all around her now.

The last thing she heard before consciousness departed from her forever was Seer Jonah laughing and saying, "Wonderful, the portal is now open."

CHAPTER 8

Liz

Liz first woke up at 2:30 am. She grinned at Melody, who was sleeping peacefully beside her, rolled over on her side, and instantly fell asleep again.

She began to dream. At first, she was in the house. And then the house altered, and she was back in Dayton, Ohio, but not in her own apartment on Cloud Park Drive. Instead, she was at her father's place down in Belmont. It was night there too and she was standing in his living room, staring out of a window at the moon above the trees. A solitary black cat creeped past on the sidewalk.

Then suddenly, Liz became aware of a commotion in the house. Somewhere in the back of it, where both her father and son were sleeping. She turned and strolled back there, parting the darkness as if it was a curtain.

Once she stepped into the hallway, the house's walls faded away from around her so that she could now see into both her son's bedroom and her father's without leaving the hallway. Both were sleeping peacefully.

And then she became aware of a scary presence. She stood in the hallway feeling frightened, but unable to determine the source of her fear. There was something terrifying nearby, but at first she couldn't see it.

And then she did see it. The house's back door suddenly bulged inward and its surface became a mess of black bubbles. There was something very nasty about these bubbles. It seemed to Liz in her dream that the bubbles were a form of evil entering the house.

The black bubbles came fully through the door and got larger and larger, and finally took on vaguely human shapes, with long and thin

54

arms and legs, and heads that were stick-like projections with bulbous eyes-on-stalks like those of snails.

There were six of these creatures and they tramped down the corridor and stepped through its invisible walls, three on either side of it.

"No, no, no!" Liz screamed as the left-hand trio of black monsters advanced on her son's bed. "Frankie, Frankie! Wake up, wake up, honey! Help me, somebody, please!"

But no help came. She wanted to run to her son's aid, but now in the dream she had no legs, her body was a pillar of flesh fused to the floor, and all she could do was watch what was going to happen.

She glanced once into her father's bedroom. Maybe alerted by her screams, he was out of bed and was facing down the black inky intruders with his shotgun in hand. The first shotgun blast splattered one of the black monsters to a pulp against the wall. But as the black jelly ran down over a photograph of her dead mother it reformed itself again.

Undeterred by this, her father had meanwhile shot another of the creatures, this time aiming for its head. The creature slumped to the floor like an emptied sack, but Liz didn't see what happened to it next.

Frankie, Frankie! she remembered and turned to look at her son, already aware of an intense struggle happening on his bed.

Now she gasped. She was just in time to see one of the black creatures forcing its way into her son's mouth. Something like black licorice was also entering Frankie's left ear. The black thing was split into seven or eight tendrils that flailed like whips as they squirmed their way into the little boy's head.

The third black monster seemed to be entering Frankie's body between his legs.

Loud thunderous noises reverberated behind Liz, but she paid no attention to them. Her entire focus was on her son and she stretched out her hands towards him, desperate to save him from this terrifying assault by these phantoms. But it was no use. She watched as the first creature's two feet slid down into Frankie's mouth, forcing his lips wide apart and bulging out his cheeks; and then watched her son swallow, gulping the monster down and afterwards licking his lips as if it were a delicious meal.

The other two creatures had already vanished into his body, and she, a distraught mother, was left with the clear knowledge that one of the creatures was now in her son's brain, one was in his belly, and the last was in his crotch. She didn't know why though.

But her child wasn't dead. All of a sudden Frankie sat up in bed. Next, he got out of bed, crossed the bedroom and walked through the wall, across the hallway and into her father's bedroom, from where the gunshot sounds had now stopped coming.

Liz now saw why the noises had stopped. Her father had been subdued by the creatures. She couldn't even see his shotgun anymore. Two of the monsters had him by his arms while the third one was trying to worm its way into his mouth, but the old man keep biting it and spitting it out.

A fresh surge of terror went through Liz at the revolting sight.

"Leave my dad alone!" she yelled at the creatures, once more powerless to intervene in what she was watching. "Yeah, fight 'em, dad!"

And it got even worse. As she watched, her own son, his previously light-brown eyes now as black as coals, strode over to his fighting grandpa, his body growing larger and larger as he went, until finally he was over seven feet tall and towered over the old man, with his blonde hair brushing the bedroom ceiling and leaving black smears on its white surface.

Then laughing like he was playing a game, he reached out and snatched the old man away from the monsters.

The old man had been able to resist the black creatures, but now he meekly gaped up in confusion at his transformed grandchild, while Frankie hugged him close and drooled on him and giggled idiotically.

Frankie seemed content to play with his grandfather in this way, but the black creatures keep jabbing their fingers at him and gabbling loudly. Strange indecipherable words came from their mouths, words that sounded like the crackling of a forest fire. And, as if he understood them, Frankie nodded and laughed some more.

Sensing that something evil was about to happen to him, granddad began trying to get free from his grandson. But his efforts were futile, his arthritis-withered old-man's strength no match for the giant kid's iron-like grip.

"Don't you dare do it!" Liz yelled at her son. "Don't you dare hurt your granddad!" She felt as terrified as her father.

But her warning fell on deaf ears, and Frankie, her transformed Frankie, ripped her father's head off of his shoulders as easily as she used to twist the heads off of her dolls when she was a little girl.

Blood spurted up into the air and hit Frankie in the face. The giant kid opened his mouth and drank the blood down. When he was tired of drinking his grandfather's blood, he handed the headless body to the black monsters so that they could drink too.

Liz screamed and fainted.

Then she woke up trembling, her breasts rising and falling with her exaggerated breathing.

She quickly realized that she'd merely been dreaming. But, bar none, this was the worst nightmare of her life. And it had seemed so real, so damn real.

She looked over at her bedmate. Melody was still fast asleep. In fact, as Liz watched her, Melody rolled over onto her back, parted her pretty lips and began snoring gently. She looked so unperturbed and so beautiful like that, that Liz felt a surge of intense and genuine affection toward her.

But then her mind returned to her own worries, to her horrible nightmare.

It's this house, this damn house, she thought as her pulse rate returned to normal. *This damn house is doing something to me. First, of course, I had my own suspicions about this place, and then I saw the pentagram carved into the balcony and next I also thought I saw a bright orange glow like a fire out on the balcony, but when Melody and I peeked out of the window there was nothing burning out there. And now I'm dreaming of monsters attacking my father and son.*

The clock on the wall informed her that the time was 4 a.m.

For a moment she considered picking up her phone and calling her father to make sure that he and Frankie were okay. But then she scowled:

This house is really affecting me badly. It's all the power of suggestion though, and I need to get a grip on myself. Yes, I know that Drake was into lots of crazy occult nonsense but I can't let that knowledge affect me like this. I have to see this through to the end. Because I really do think now that Drake knows how to cure Frankie of his autism.

Taking care not to wake Melody, Liz got out of bed to use the bathroom. Then she returned to bed and fell asleep again.

Through the rest of the night Liz tossed and turned restlessly in the grip of horrible dreams.

CHAPTER 9

Nick

When Nick Sinclair awoke that morning, he at first thought that something was wrong with his wristwatch.

One of the first things Nick did each morning was to step up to his bedroom window and throw open the drapes. It was almost a religious ritual to him: letting the new day in, as it were.

And so this morning too, Nick got out of bed, walked over to the window, and pulled back its green curtains. Then he stared out at the slate-grey sky in confusion.

His confusion wasn't deep at first, just a niggling feeling that something wasn't right; a subconscious bother that refused to go away.

Part of the problem was that Nick generally woke up at around the same time each day, normally at 7 a.m. Nick lived in the Boston neighborhood of Dorchester, a reasonable distance from work, and his internal clock had figured out for him that waking up at 7 a.m. each day gave him more than enough time to bathe, have coffee and toast, and make it to the office on time.

So today, with this being the summer, when the days were naturally longer, Nick felt that the sky should have been much brighter by now.

He looked back at the bed. Todd was still asleep, facing the other way with one hand dangling over the bed's edge.

Nick walked over to the nightstand, picked up his phone, and checked the time. It confirmed what his watch said; the time was supposedly 7:23 a.m. now, which, considering the amount of time he'd been standing by the window, seemed just right to him.

Nick shrugged off his unease. *Maybe there's a storm on the way, or clouds have covered the sun. It's real weird though; real unusual.*

He turned towards a sound on the other side of the bed. Todd was awake now, sitting up and rubbing his eyes with the backs of his hands.

When Todd finally noticed Nick, he said, "Dude, I can't wait to be out of this damn house. You wouldn't believe the crazy dreams I had tonight." He grimaced as if the nightmares were replaying in his mind. Then he asked, "What's up with you? You look worried about something."

Nick shook his head. "I guess it's nothing really. But I've got this feeling that something's wrong."

Todd nodded knowingly. "Did you dream too?"

Nick nodded back. "Yeah, I did, and it wasn't pretty either." He considered telling Todd what he'd dreamt. In Nick's nightmare, he'd been trapped in a giant library, one that had seemed to contain all of the most evil books in the universe, and he'd had to read through them all to find the key to open the library door so he could escape and return home again. And meanwhile there were odd monsters, like ink blots with stick limbs, watching him and shuffling the volumes around to confuse and frustrate him. And other monsters stalked the aisles between the bookcases, with plans to corrupt him so he became one of them.

He decided the dream would just seem silly to Todd. "But it's not the dream bothering me. It's something else. I mean—"

"Hey, is there gonna be a thunderstorm?" Todd interrupted him. "Sky seems dark as hell out there."

"That's part of the problem . . . the sky . . . it's . . ."

But he needn't have bothered explaining. Todd was already up and out of bed and shambling over to the green drapes on the other side of the bedroom. (As if in compensation for the space eaten up by the rear balcony, both upstairs bedrooms extended from the front to the back of the house.)

After spending a few seconds scratching the dark hair on his bare chest, Todd pulled the drapes apart and stared outside. Then he gave a start and stiffened, the muscles in his back visibly contracting.

Watching him freeze like that, Nick felt his worries return. If Nick had noticed something wrong too . . .

"Hey, dude, get over here right now." Todd wasn't requesting that Nick join him at the window; he was demanding it, the way an army sergeant might order a private to get a move on. He didn't look back at Nick as he spoke. In fact, he seemed unable to move from his position by the window. And his voice sounded scared, as if he was only a few degrees away from cracking up.

Nick didn't bother asking why Todd was calling him over to the window. All he knew was that something outside the house had scared Todd, who'd always seemed impervious to fear. And if battle-scarred Todd Wilson was scared, then they definitely had a problem.

So Nick shambled around the bed and walked over to Todd's side. "Look," Todd said.

Nick looked. At first he didn't get it. He stared up at the sky. It was as gravel-gray as before, which was mainly odd because, now that he really paid attention to it, there were no thunderheads in evidence. In fact, there were lots of equally gray clouds floating across the heavens.

"Yeah, man, I already noticed that the sky looks weird."

"Not *up*, dude. Look *down*."

Nick looked down and immediately saw what Todd meant. "Oh! What happened to the house opposite?" he asked in shock, because Nick clearly remembered that when they'd arrived here yesterday evening, there had been a cute brown building with white windows and doors standing opposite. Now he was staring at ruins over there, at desolation that might have been fresh when his father was born.

Todd was still frozen beside him. "Something's happened," he said. "Something really bad has happened here. That house didn't look like that yesterday. When we got down from our car, I recall looking back across the road and seeing a silver car parked outside it. A blonde woman was getting out of the car, and a kid was opening the front door and . . ."

"Yeah, but what . . . what . . . what . . . what the hell?" Nick felt it begin now, a cold feeling trickling down his spine. This wasn't like his normal gut feeling that something was about to go wrong with a reporting assignment. He'd had those plenty of times, and had come to respect them when they occurred. But the way he felt now—looking across the road at the mausoleum-like structure that had somehow replaced the family house previously situated opposite? Well, it felt like someone—God maybe—had exploded a bomb in his soul.

Oh, this is bad. Bad as hell.

The sky hadn't changed a bit. It was still that weird half-daylight tone, a gray background that suited the wrecked building they were staring at.

And there was more to see. Nick finally tore his eyes from the most obvious difference out there and began noticing the other glaring abnormalities about the scene.

The trees, for instance. This area of Raynham had lots of trees. Actually, as a rule, Raynham seemed to have more trees than people. And this being summer, those trees had had lush foliage, as if they'd been giving it their best shot at having a botanic fashion parade before the fall season forced them to strip naked again.

But now . . .

All the trees were withered and sickly. Not dead or dying. No . . . they looked the way trees looked when the soil was poor, or if . . . if they never got enough sunlight. Nick studied the trees' yellow leaves and then gazed down at the piss-amber grass on the front lawn, which seemed as sickly as the trees did. Once more he felt that bomb-like surge of fear.

He looked up at the sky.

"Do you think the sky *here* is always like that?" Todd asked.

"Here? *Here?* What the hell do you mean by *here*, man?" Taking a very deep breath to prevent himself from screaming, Nick turned to look at Todd. Then he repeated his question, slowly letting out each word at a sane pitch that completely belied his actual state of mind. "Yeah, what exactly do you mean . . . *here?*"

Todd seemed to have gotten over his shock. "Well, we definitely aren't where we went to sleep last night. Maybe we were drugged and moved someplace else while we slept."

Nick calmed himself too. He didn't bother replying Todd's suggestion that they'd been moved while they slept. He didn't believe a word of it and suspected Todd didn't either. That explanation was merely something to say to stave off the threat of encroaching insanity. Yes, it was possible that there could be two identical houses and they'd been kidnapped and shunted from one to the other. But the world outside couldn't be faked.

Then Nick looked out of the window again and did another sharp intake of breath. "What the hell is that?"

Todd looked out too and gasped. "Dude, I don't think that's a bird. It looks more like a man . . . or a woman . . . with wings. Someone flying in the sky. . . . Aw, heck!"

The winged apparition vanished off to their right. Todd looked back in at Nick and they both stared at each other in horror, neither of them able to form words.

At that moment they heard a loud yell. Then another. Then began a whole lot of shouting.

Nick managed a wry smile. "Man, I think the girls have just made the same observations we have."

Todd nodded. "And all the noise is coming from downstairs, meaning they're letting that Seer Jonah freak know exactly how they feel."

Then there was a knock on their bedroom door.

Todd looked at Nick. "Who's that?"

"Most likely Chloe, come to fetch us," Nick replied. He looked over at the door and called out, "Come in, it's unlocked!"

The door clicked open and Chloe stepped inside the bedroom. She looked as confused as they did; shock was etched all over her pretty face and her blonde hair was as tangled as a bird's nest, like she was too confused to make herself look presentable. Nick noted that she was wearing the same jeans and tee-shirt as yesterday, as if she'd fallen asleep in her clothes.

"Guys, have you looked outside the house?" she gasped breathlessly as she hurried towards them. "It's . . . it's . . . *everything is different* out there now. I-I-I . . . we-we . . . we don't know wh-wh-where we are now."

Nick gestured to the window. "That's exactly what we're discussing at the moment. Hey, what's happening downstairs? What's all the noise about?"

Todd nodded. Chloe explained: "The wives are demanding that Seer Jonah explain what's going on."

"And . . . ?" Nick asked.

Chloe shrugged. "He said to fetch you guys first, that he'll explain to all of us over breakfast; that way he won't have to do it twice."

Nick scowled. "Breakfast? Is the guy crazy? How the hell am I supposed to have any appetite with winged people flying past the house?"

Chloe's eyes widened and she trembled. "Winged people?" She hurried to the window and looked out. "Where are they?"

"Gone, thankfully," Todd replied. "But there was a winged woman out there." He waited till Chloe turned away from facing the window, then said, "Well, let's do what the tattooed man says: head downstairs and hear his explanation for this madness." He forced a laugh as he walked over to the closet and pulled his shirt off a hanger. "Hopefully, it'll be something as mundane as him having put LSD in our drinks last night."

Nick watched him dress; the bullet scars in his belly were brown stiches against his sunburned torso. "Hey, you brought your gun, right?"

Todd nodded. "Never leave home without it. You know I'm always prepared for stuff like this." Leaving his shirt unbuttoned he began fishing in his equipment bag.

Nick looked at Chloe. "You packing too on this trip?"

She shook her head. "It never occurred to me that we might be in danger. Drake's my brother; he'd never hurt me."

Todd pulled out his gun—a large Glock—and frowned at her. "It ain't your brother I'm worried about, girl, it's that freak down there with 'I WILL SAVE YOU' tattooed on his face. I don't like or trust that guy. If he's the real deal, I suspect he's what would have resulted if Hitler and Liz Bathory ever had kids."

Nick looked up from pulling his shoes on. "C'mon, man, don't sensationalize things. This is worrying enough already."

Chloe had meanwhile sat down on the bed to wait for them to get ready. She'd left the bedroom door open and they could hear the noise from downstairs. The noise was entirely female and came in short passionate bursts. Nick figured that the pauses in between each feminine outburst was Seer Jonah trying to explain something to Liz and Melody Melville.

"What're the wives so pissed off about?"

"Bonnie's missing," Chloe explained, fright written all over her face.

"What?" Todd ejected the magazine from the grip of the Glock, examined its content of slugs, and then slipped it back into the grip. He smiled coldly as the magazine clicked back into place, then slid back the slide to cock it. "Well, I'm ready to rock and roll."

Nick realized that the warrior in Todd had just come to the fore. Which was great, because personally he was at a loss for what to do. If only Chloe had brought her gun. *But she's right. Drake's her brother and from all accounts the guy loves her like mad.* Then he looked out of the window and seconded Todd's stated worry: *Only, it ain't Drake we've got to worry about now. I mean, where the hell are we?*

He stared oddly at Chloe: "What's that again about Bonnie having gone missing?"

CHAPTER 10

Chloe

"I woke up this morning and Bonnie hadn't come to bed," Chloe explained while watching the men dress. "I knew she hadn't, because she was gonna bring in our bags when coming to the bedroom. So then I shrugged it off; at this point I hadn't yet looked out of the windows and seen the changes outside. I just assumed that Bonnie had done some late drinking and passed out in front of the TV set while watching a movie. But then I went out to the living room to look for her and she wasn't there. Nor was any of her stuff."

Chloe paused and looked at both men's faces, while jabbing fingers into her blonde hair and scratching her scalp. She was long overdue a visit to the hair salon. As she'd expected would be the case, Nick looked confused, while Todd already looked ready to shoot someone. "So then," she went on, 'I began picking up my bags and stuff off of the chairs. Once I'd collected all my things, I went into the kitchen to retrieve my cellphone from the top of the kitchen counter. Seer Jonah was in the kitchen cooking breakfast, so I said hello. And I also asked him where Bonnie was. At this time I still thought that maybe . . . maybe she'd gone upstairs to sleep in Liz and Melody's room."

She frowned. "But then Seer Jonah told me that Bonnie had called a Uber at around midnight and left for a friend's place in Boston. According to him, she was quite drunk and was claiming that Liz had broken her heart." She nodded at Nick. "I guess you were right about her wanting to bang Liz."

"And Liz went to bed with Melody instead," Todd said, clearly not originally aware of all the sexual tension that had been in the air last night, but fast catching on. "Or at least they slept in the same bed." He nodded and frowned. "Okay, I get that much. It makes sense to me that Bonnie would leave if she caught the wives screwing themselves." He glanced at Nick to see what Nick thought.

Nick nodded. "I agree. It makes perfect sense that Bonnie would get pissed off and leave." Then he grimaced and gestured at the bedroom door, through which they could hear Liz Melville yelling something, though her actual words were indistinct. "So what's the ruckus about?"

Chloe shrugged. "It's mostly fear—Liz letting off steam. Maybe they wouldn't have gotten so worked up, but when Jonah finished telling them about Bonnie's departure, Melody jokingly remarked that maybe he'd sacrificed her to create this damn mess we're now in? Liz caught onto that and she's been close to raving mad ever since." Chloe paused in her narration and smirked. "And yes, I do think the pair of them had sex last night. They're acting suspiciously chummy this morning."

"That's your brother's problem," Nick said with a grin. "The first law of divorce and remarriage is to keep ex-new and new wife as far separated as possible, 'cos if you don't, they'll go at it tooth-and-nail and you'll be in the middle getting scratched; though in this case, it seems they've turned into lovers, not fighters."

"Yeah, something like that," Chloe agreed. "And you're right, it is Drake's prob—"

She shut up then because a winged person was flying past the window; a man wearing blue clothes. Chloe gasped and pointed. Nick had also noticed the passing man, but Todd turned too late to catch the strange sight.

"It was another flyer!" Chloe explained to Todd, her whole body now shivering from her head to her hush puppies. "Guys, I feel like I'm going mad! Either that or I'm still fast asleep downstairs and I need someone to wake me up already!"

"Guys," Todd said, tucking his gun into the rear waistband of his jeans and letting the hem of his shirt fall over it, "let's head downstairs and hear what Seer Jonah has to say about all this."

***

Chloe and the other five sat around the breakfast table, which had already been set when she'd brought the men downstairs. Seer Jonah had once again laid out a sumptuous spread: hot toast, scrambled eggs and bacon, tea and coffee, butter and cheese, strawberry and blueberry jams, a large bowl of mixed nuts, and a much larger bowl of fruit. A lot more food than they could eat.

Chloe wondered if maybe the food was poisoned. *Maybe I'll crack into a nut or bite an apple and next thing I'll fall asleep and wake up . . . where?*

As if the presence of the others had reduced her fright, Liz was silent now, occupied with buttering a slice of toast, with Melody occasionally whispering in her ear.

Yeah, no doubt about it. Those two had sex last night.

Neither Nick nor Todd had served themselves any food. Chloe had a slice of toast on her plate, but couldn't decide what she wanted with it.

"Eat, eat," Seer Jonah urged everyone. "As you can see, there's more than enough for us all."

"Dude we just want to know what the hell is going on here," Todd growled back at him. Chloe recognized that tone of voice: Todd was getting really upset, and with that gun he was carrying, Seer Jonah was in dire danger of the ex-marine filling him full of holes.

Their seating arrangement around the table matched last night's, with Chloe and her friends on one side of the table and Liz, Melody and Seer Jonah on the other. The latter trio were arranged in that order, with Liz seated opposite Todd, Melody opposite Nick, and Seer Jonah seated directly opposite Chloe, which she felt might be the reason her appetite had fled to parts unknown. Looking at Seer Jonah's hairless and tattooed face filled her with the impression that she'd stepped wholesale into a nightmare. Recalling his face's tar-like transformation in the cleaver blade last night merely bolstered this impression.

The dining room drapes were wide open, affording them all a disconcerting view of the new landscape outside, where the trees all looked like they were dying and the grass looked jaundiced, and where the sky was that impossible gray and the sun that hung near the horizon didn't appear to have moved an inch in the past hour.

Chloe had the sudden unnerving feeling that she was about to become religious in a big way. The sun in the sky looked like God's eye.

But despite seeing all of this, Chloe still had no idea what was going on. And for a reporter this was worse than frustrating.

"Yeah, dude," Nick told Seer Jonah, as if he'd read her thoughts. "What the hell is going on here? What have you done to us?"

Seer Jonah drank some coffee and grinned broadly. "Ladies and gentlemen, there's really no need for you to get annoyed. You came here to meet with Mr. Melville and I assure you that once breakfast is over, I'll take you across town to meet with him."

Chloe mused on this statement. "But . . ." she said slowly, choosing her words with care, "this clearly isn't where we arrived to yesterday. Would you mind telling us where we are now? There are winged people flying around outside."

Melody and Liz both looked startled at that info. "Winged people?"

Chloe nodded at them. "Yeah, a winged man flew past the house five minutes ago. And according to Todd and Nick, they'd already seen a winged woman do the same." She stared coldly at Seer Jonah. "So, man, I'm really running out of patience. Where exactly are we now?"

Seer Jonah nodded. "Alright, I promised you all an explanation and you'll have it." He grinned like a wolf. "How familiar are you all with the concept of parallel universes . . . or in this case, parallel Earths?"

Chloe and her companions stared at him in equal shock, although Chloe, having watched the same sci-fi blockbusters as everyone else, now realized she'd been expecting and dreading an explanation like this.

"We're on a parallel Earth?" she finally asked, when everyone else still appeared shell-shocked. Liz seemed particularly affected by the news: her mouth hung open and a piece of toast hung precariously on her tongue.

"Yes," Seer Jonah said. "If you've read Mr. Melville's book, and I think you all have, then you're already familiar with his descriptions of this place."

He rose to his feet and spread his arms wide in a dramatic gesture. "Ladies and gentlemen, I welcome you all to the Static Earth."

"Oh shit, no!" Chloe gasped and looked around at the others in a dawning horror that was clearly reflected back on their own faces.

CHAPTER 11

The Static Earth

Simply put, the Static Earth was the regular Earth's evil twin.

'Static' in this case referred to the fact that this particular version of the Earth had stopped spinning.

This cessation of rotational motion had nothing to do with either the planet's age or some sort of global or cosmic cataclysm, like a nuclear war for instance.

No, magical forces of almost inconceivable magnitude were responsible for the Static Earth's current miserable state.

The short version of the story was simply that 500 years ago the wizard Bolok, a vassal of Lord Norgem, had on his master's instructions, sought to raise from the bottom of the northern Atlantic Ocean the ancient sunken land of Hedaye, a continent-sized area of the seabed exactly corresponding to the regular Earth's location of the fabled kingdom of Atlantis.

Given the choice between draining the sun of energy to accomplish this task and leeching the Earth of its rotational force, the wizard Bolok wisely decided the latter was safer. And so Hedaye was raised to the ocean surface and the Earth's spin was slowed down to a halt, a process that took five years to accomplish.

The most obvious result of the Static Earth's motionless state was that now one side of the planet existed in permanent night and the other in permanent daylight; both sides being separated by a zone of permanent twilight.

Ironically, the previously sunken land of Hedaye (aka Atlantis) which was responsible for all this madness now lay on the planet's darkside, as did the area ruled by the monarch—Lord Norgem— who'd ordered the evil deed done; an area those in the other Earth called Germany.

Other than for Hedaye's existence, however, the Static Earth was an exact duplicate of the normal, spinning Earth, with continents, countries, and even towns existing in exactly the same location on each.

This meant that it was easy to slip from one world to the other if you knew how. (And Drake Melville clearly knew how.)

In many cases even, the same people were duplicated in both versions of the planet—the static and the spinning—and adventurers who crossed over from one to the other found themselves in danger of being accused of identity theft.

As to how such a strange duplicate of the rotating planet had come to be in the first place, no one—not even the clone world's thousands of sorcerers—had a damn clue.

Shit happens even in the wider universe, it seems. The fans it hits are merely bigger.

A secondary difference between the spinning and static earths was in the nature of their technologies. Most of the Static Earth ran on magic. Sorcery was their electricity; magicians, witches and warlocks their Nobel-prize-winning scientists. Literally.

And these Static Earth 'scientists,' while performing their diabolical research like all scientists do, had both intentionally and unwittingly unleashed strange and incredible things on their world and its hapless inhabitants.

And so, now the Static Earth was a place where nightmares walked in plain daylight, where impossible creatures stalked the eight continents' immense forests of withered trees and jaundiced grass. Frog-like monsters that dwarfed blue whales in size (and ate them for breakfast) swam the oceans. Winged people, carnivorous birds the size of aircraft, monstrous dragons, and acid-dripping tentacled things even more deadly than those flew the never-changing dark or light skies.

This was the sort of confusing place where one might meet an angel or demon drinking at one's local bar, or find an incubus or succubus in one's bed. Sometimes the demonic sex workers even serviced one free of charge.

Or one might even meet an alien shopping at Walmart, if its starship had crash-landed and it had no way to phone home.

But the majority of people on the static Earth were human and for the most part, the planet looked just like the regular Earth. And one way or another, the other Earth's inventions had bled through into the magic, so that they were mostly up-to-date on modern technology: aircraft, automobiles, telecoms, computers—they had it all; except that much of it was powered not by gasoline or electricity or solar energy, but by magical biotechnology.

And so, once a traveler between the realms got over the oddity of their translocation, he or she (or it) could more-or-less adapt easily to living on the Static Earth.

If, that is, 1) a monster didn't eat them first, or 2) they didn't get blown up in a war between two rival countries or 3) and most ironic of all . . . their own doppelganger didn't kill them, enraged by their perceived identity theft.

Which neatly returns one to the story, to the quintet of perplexed listeners to Seer Jonah's explanation of their very baffling new location . . .

CHAPTER 12

Liz

"I don't believe this for one damn minute," Melody whispered to Liz, while beside them Seer Jonah ranted on about how the Static Earth was exactly like the Earth they knew except that it had stopped spinning, and that here magic was a tangible force that one could harness and use, just like electricity was in their home plane. And how—and of more immediate concern to all those gathered at the breakfast table—this house was currently acting as a gateway or portal between both worlds, with its opening now in the Static Earth.

"Can't say I want to believe him either," Liz whispered back with a shiver. "But if there really are flying people up in the air outside, I suggest we listen to him."

"This is a very evil and dangerous place," the tattooed man went on. "But, thankfully, you won't be going to the evil and dangerous places. As previously arranged by Mr. Drake, I'll merely take you across town to where he's waiting for you. And afterwards you'll drive straight back here. No sightseeing on this tour, folks."

"Say we assume for a moment that you're actually telling us the truth and not bullshitting us," Todd said, "what's the name of this town we're now in?"

"Why, Raynham of course."

"Raynham?"

Seer Jonah nodded. "Yes, most places here have exactly the same names and in some places, the same people living in them. You might even meet yourself here, which can be rather disconcerting."

"Total B.S.," Melody whispered to Liz. "I hate this sci-fi crap."

In contrast to Melody, Liz Melville would have *loved* to disbelieve Seer Jonah's explanation. But she'd experienced so much strangeness while married to Drake, that she knew she'd be extremely foolish to doubt what the tattooed man was saying.

Two days ago Frankie suddenly became well again and told me to come here and now I'm here and . . .

Here? Her thoughts stalled as she looked out of the window. *According to this guy we're all now stuck in a place that the rest of the world thinks is mere fiction. This is just crazy, completely nutty.*

The reason Liz had earlier been raging at Seer Jonah was because she'd discovered that her cellphone wasn't working. She'd wanted to call her father. She'd tried borrowing Melody's phone but it had no network signal either. Neither phone had had any signal bars at all.

It was like that time when she'd gone to film part of her TV series on Misery Mountain, out in the western part of Massachusetts, right on the state line. The chopper had dropped she and the film crew on the mountain peak and then, staring down from that dizzying height into the state of New York, Liz had suddenly remembered that Frankie had a noon appointment with his pediatrician at the Dayton Children's Hospital. She'd tried to call his caregiver Mrs. Bergman, to remind her to drive him to the clinic. But they'd been so far up Misery Mountain that no one's phone had picked up a signal. In the end she'd had to ask the departing helicopter pilot to make the call for her when he got back to Ohio.

If that had been frustrating, this was much more so; particularly after the night's nightmare of black monsters attacking her father and her son.

She shuddered as she remembered her horrible dream, and its equally horrible ending—Frankie's transformation into a giant cretin who'd then murdered his grandfather. It was her need to make a phone call that had brought her downstairs, where she'd met a very scared Chloe asking Seer Jonah how the building across the road had suddenly collapsed and aged forty or so years overnight.

She remembered she was supposed to be eating breakfast, so she shoved some toast in her mouth and began chewing it slowly, while listening to the question Nick was asking Seer Jonah:

"So what were those creatures? I mean, those flying people outside?"

Seer Jonah made a dismissive gesture towards the open dining room windows. "Oh those? They're called angelus."

"They're angels?" Melody asked.

Seer Jonah shook his head. "No, they are not angels. Except for their wings, the angelus are as human as you and I." He smiled. "There's a joke about the angelus, which says that their name is a combination of 'angel' and 'jealous,' because, not being immortal themselves, they're envious of God's angels, who are."

"Are they dangerous?" Melody asked. Her right hand was squeezing Liz's left hand under the table. Liz could feel the transsexual woman's legs trembling too.

And I thought I was the scared one, she mused. *But maybe all the shouting I did earlier helped ease the accelerator pedal off of my fear. I feel quite calm now. Well about as calm as anyone who knows they're out of their depth can possibly feel.*

To use an acting simile, she felt like she was performing in a movie written by her ex-husband, but one without a script; like she was improvising her character's actions, and making up her lines on the fly.

Under the table, she squeezed Melody's thigh comfortingly. She still felt warmth towards the woman from last night's sexual encounter, and thankfully, this morning's insane revelations hadn't entirely muddied the sheen of those delicious memories.

But it would have been nicer if Bonnie hadn't deserted us like this. Soon Melody and Drake are gonna be reunited and I'll be on my own again.

"No, angelus aren't dangerous," Seer Jonah replied Melody. "Well, not unless you piss them off. Then they can really be a pain in your ass. Otherwise they mind their own business, same as everyone else does around here. Those you earlier spotted were most likely on their way to work."

"How long until the cycle spins back to our own world again?" Chloe asked. "I mean, when does the portal reopen? When can we leave this creepy place?"

Seer Jonah shrugged. "About four hours, more or less." He looked around at them all. "That's more than sufficient time for us to drive across town and return. You'll have enough time to see Drake, interview him, and return home safely." His gaze turned from Drake's sister to the two other women. "Of course, both Misses Melvilles may wish to stay longer, to discuss personal matters with their husband."

Liz rolled her eyes. "I really wish you'd stop saying that," she told Seer Jonah. "Can't you just remember that I'm divorced from Drake?"

"My apologies. I'll try to keep it in mind from now on," the man replied. "But I think you get what I mean. If either of you wish to remain behind, that is fine too. You can always leave during another cycle—"

"Hell no, we ain't going nowhere," Todd interrupted him.

Liz winced when she saw the gun the cameraman was pointing at Seer Jonah.

"Dude, I don't trust you one bit," Todd went on. "And so I think the smart thing for all of us to do is to sit right here and wait out the next four hours for your so-called cycle to complete itself; so we can return back to where we came from. Personally, I've had enough of this shit already."

On seeing the gun, Melody began laughing. "Oh Jesus, this is insane!"

"Put your gun away, Mr. Wilson," Seer Jonah said calmly, without giving the slightest hint that he felt intimidated by the weapon. "I understand that you're worried and scared, but shooting me won't help matters any."

"And why the hell do you think that is?" Todd asked angrily. "Like I already told you, I don't trust you an inch. I don't know what setup you've got going here, but I sure as hell want out of it as soon as possible. So like I just said, we're gonna sit right here for the next four hours, until your so-called 'time-space portal' opens again, and then we're all gonna just walk out the front door, get into our cars, and drive off back the way we came. Personally, I say to hell with interviewing Drake Melville. This is too strange already." He swung the gun up as Seer Jonah made to leave his seat. "Hell no, asshole, don't you dare. You make one wrong move now and I'll blow your head off. And then we'll all still sit here and wait till the countdown is up, only you won't be around to see the portal open again. "

The tattooed man sat down again. He shook his head. "Actually you can't shoot me."

Todd smirked at him. "Oh yeah? Dude, maybe you should enlighten me as to why not?"

With a frown on his face that quickly became an unpleasant smile, Seer Jonah leaned forward over the breakfast table, in the process almost overturning the large fruit bowl. "Because, when the cycle completes, the portal won't open except I recite a spell, an unlocking key." He leaned back in his seat and stared coldly around the table.

"So you see, everyone, you need me alive to go back home. If anything happens to me you'll all be trapped here forever. Not even Mr. Melville himself knows how to unlock the portal back to the Spinning Earth."

Liz doubted that this last was true. *Drake got in here, didn't he?* But at the moment she didn't feel like taking chances.

"Hey, Todd, please put the gun away," she said airily, hoping that her seeming lack of concern would help defuse the tense situation.

For a moment it seemed like her plan wouldn't work, but then Todd sighed and looked sideways at Nick. Nick nodded back at him. Todd lowered his gun, then told Seer Jonah, "Just remember, dude, that I got my eyes on you twenty-four-seven. The others may have bought that story about Bonnie going home, but I still think it's dodgy. But for the moment I'm give you the benefit of the doubt. You screw with us however, and I will blow your head off."

"Todd, *please* put the gun away," Chloe pleaded in a nervous voice. "Let's all just do like Mr. Jonah says, get this over with quickly and go home again. This isn't somewhere that I wanna be for longer than I can help."

"Okay, okay," Todd agreed, wagging a finger at Seer Jonah. "Just remember—I'm watching you. One suspicious move from you and you ain't gonna have no head no more."

"I won't forget it," Seer Jonah said just as coldly.

And staring at him, Liz felt startled for a moment. *Hey, did his red tattoos just glow angrily as he spoke?*

"Oh enough, enough already with the 'tough guy' posturing, both of you!" Melody exclaimed.

She waited until Todd had put the gun away, and then added, "I suggest we all finish this delicious breakfast Seer Jonah made, and then go find Drake. I for one can't wait to see my darling again. Oh, it's been so damn long since I felt a nice hard cock up my ass!"

An awkward silence filled the dining room after her statement.

"Oh, I guess the cat's out of the bag now as to why you want to see him so badly," Seer Jonah said with a knowing smirk.

"Cat out of the bag? More like the dick's out of the fag," Liz said without thinking, and then instantly covered her mouth and giggled. "Sorry, girl, I honestly didn't mean to say that. It just slipped out. Honest."

"Oh, no offense taken, honey," Melody said with a giggle of her own. "The dick has been out of this fag for way too long now and I want it back in there soonest." She looked around at the men and then pouted sexily. "So . . . can we all eat our breakfast like good adults, and then go find my wayward husband, please?"

"And my wayward ex?" Liz added sweetly.

"Yeah, of course," Nick, Todd, and Chloe instantly agreed, clearly desperate to be spared further embarrassing conversation.

Breakfast continued without incident after that.

Welcome to Drake's Static Earth, folks, Liz thought glumly, as scary images from Drake's novel began trickling into her mind. *What in the world will happen to us now?*

CHAPTER 13

Nick

They drove off from the house in both cars. Melody's BMW SUV led the way. Seer Jonah rode with her and Liz.

Todd drove the blue Ford sedan behind the brown SUV. Nick was riding shotgun beside him while Chloe owned the backseat.

Nick looked back at Chloe and shook his head in amusement. She was still fiddling with her cellphone, sweeping it through the air and trying to get a signal.

She noticed Nick watching her and scowled in disgust. "Nothing," she said. "Absolutely nothing. I just can't believe it."

Nick nodded in sympathy. He and Todd had also tested their phones with similar results.

Seer Jonah's explanation had seemed logical enough: "There's nothing wrong with your phones," he'd explained. "They're still working perfectly. You're just not subscribed to any of the phone networks here."

Which made sense, Nick agreed, so long as they accepted the basic fact that they were no longer on Earth as they knew it.

Chloe finally got tired of searching for a network signal. She stowed her phone back into her purse and stared out of the window instead.

"This place," she said a few seconds later. "It's just crazy that we're here now."

Nick turned away from her and resumed staring out of the windshield. Aside from the gray sky, there was very little out of the ordinary to see. Apparently, the ruined house opposite Drake's place which had alerted them to the changes in their location was a singular occurrence. Most of this town they were driving through—this alternate Raynham—looked exactly like the Raynham they'd traversed yesterday. Well more-or-less so.

Chloe suddenly yelped, "Hey look! There's another one of them now! Wow!"

It took Nick a few moments to realize that she'd sighted another of the angelus.

Nick studied the flying man. Or was that a woman up there? At that height and speed it was impossible to make out the flying person's gender; he or she was just an elongated shape in brown pants and tee shirt and with flapping wings. Also, this angelus seemed to be dark-skinned. The previous two Nick had seen had had pale skin.

"Hey, honey, control yourself, wilya?" Todd grunted from behind the steering wheel, after Chloe's surprised yelp almost made him veer across the street into the path of an oncoming truck. These were the first words he'd spoken since they'd set out from the house. The ex-marine's jaw muscles were bunched up tight, his lips were set in a grim line, and his Glock pistol now rested in his lap; which gave Nick major cause for concern if the police here stopped them.

Chloe had gone quiet. When Nick twisted in his seat to stare at her, she waved off the concerned look in his eyes. "Oh, I'll be alright now," she said. "This stuff just takes getting used to. Like falling into a movie, you know?"

"I don't wanna get used to it," Todd said. "All I wanna do now is record the footage of your brother and get out of here."

"C'mon, man, lighten up a little," Nick said. "Hey, Todd, just tell me this isn't gonna be great when we return home. Imagine us telling everyone where we've been. We're gonna be world famous."

Todd shook his head. "Dude, I don't think it's gonna work out like that for us."

"Why not?" Chloe inquired from the backseat. "We've got definite proof here."

"Well, firstly," Todd explained, while swinging their car around a corner and accelerating to keep pace with the SUV they were following, "because our all-powerful US government will clamp down on the info. We'll all be taken into custody and threatened and warned to keep our damn mouths shut, or else . . . Hey, I've seen it happen more than once to potential whistleblowers when I was in the marines. To avoid a scandal, the top brass'll tell you to STFU, and then you're as good as hogtied—you either zip your damn lip or your career's over." He laughed bitterly. "And meanwhile of course, the gov will be trying to work out a way to leech this weird earth of its resources."

"Wow, man, I guess you're right about that," Chloe said. "And now that you mention it, who's to say that the government doesn't already know about this place anyway and has been keeping it secret from us all this while."

"Hmm, I'll second you on that," Todd agreed.

Nick had been following the conversation while staring out of the window at an approaching woman pushing a pram. She was young, pretty, and seemed completely normal; just like all the other humans he'd so far seen here.

Except for the angelus, of course.

They were driving south through the town, rolling down Broadway, and everything seemed normal enough; even the giant Walmart superstore was in the right place.

Normal, everything so damn normal, Nick thought. *Except, of course, for the unchanging sky with the sun permanently hanging over there on our right, and the sickly looking plants. The flowers here all look like they need a painter to touch them up. Oh, man, this is so weird.*

The sky was still as grey as dusk. Seer Jonah had explained that most of the east coast of the USA was in the twilight zone. The Americas had had good fortune in this regard, as most of their countries lay in the zone of daylight. Western Europe, Africa, and the Middle East had been less fortunate however: those parts of the world existed in permanent darkness. Though even in those darkside areas, if the magic was powerful enough it was possible to create small patches of localized daylight over a region.

Todd stopped at a street light and the woman with the pram walked past them, glancing into their car as she did so. Blonde, pretty, pregnant.

Looking out through the side window after her, Nick caught a brief glimpse of a bright blue bonnet in the pram she was pushing, and of a purple pacifier protruding from a tiny pink face, and of a tiny waving hand.

Normal, everything so damn normal.

Of course, the normalcy is helping us all cope with this; keeping us from freaking out.

He glanced back at Chloe again. Once more she had her phone out and seemed to be entering information into a notepad app. The expression on her face was a curious one that mingled puzzlement, excitement and fear; lots of fear in fact.

Nick repressed a sigh. He knew that facial expression well. He'd seen it times without number while he and Chloe had been dating.

***

Nick was originally from down south, Longview, Texas to be exact. After leaving university he'd drifted from profession to profession, until finally he'd become a reporter. A shrink friend of Nick's had told him that he'd wound up with the Boston Globe because journalism suited his wanderlust. Nick Sinclair wasn't the kind of personality to sit behind a desk and shuffle papers; as had been demonstrated on the two occasions that the Globe had tried to make an editor out of him. Both times he'd felt like the walls of life were closing in on him.

So maybe his wanderlust was due to claustrophobia?

But it was while stuck behind the editor's desk, trying not to go out of his damn mind, that he'd gotten close to Chloe Melville.

After a while they'd started dating. At first the romance had been great, but sadly, the relationship didn't last.

See, Chloe had deep-rooted sexual issues; deeper than the six-feet hole you buried a corpse in. Chloe's problems weren't her fault; she'd once being raped at a party.

Chloe had wept all through the time she'd been relating her ordeal to Nick. He'd sympathized and tried to be supportive, but the relationship still hadn't worked out.

Which was a crying shame, because back then he'd been convinced she was his soul mate. Even putting her natural blonde cuteness aside, he'd found her perfect for him.

Though responsive in bed, she was very passive, which he'd liked. He'd loved caressing and licking her for long stretches of time while she lay back gasping and moaning and finally pleading with him to enter and possess her. But he preferred to first make her climax with his tongue and fingers before entering her. He found her relaxed limpness in this afterglow state, the laxness of her muscles after her climax, an additional turn-on. In this state the sweaty expanse of her skin seemed to be an enemy country that he'd singlehandedly conquered.

Okay, so Todd was the combat groupie, but Nick too could occasionally manage a battlefield metaphor.

And that ass! Chloe's ass was really tight. Small but perfect. To get a proper hold of it in bed, Nick had always had to dip his fingers into her ass crack, the tips of his fingers brushing the fine hairs around her anus.

Wow, this woman's ass brainwashes me, he'd think while caressing it. *Each time I see her I feel like I'm just five seconds away from committing a rape.*

He hadn't felt that way about any of his later girlfriends. Or their asses. Which maybe was a shame, or maybe it wasn't.

But some things simply weren't meant to be. Outside of the bedroom, things were great between Nick and Chloe They worked together, laughed together, had fun together. But the bedroom was the brick wall. Not because she didn't give herself to him, but because, well . . .

Chloe's angst and anger were a deep well, and sometimes when they made love she seemed to be reliving her rape—her eyes would turn wild and she'd shove him off her and begin crying.

Nick had broken up with Chloe after she'd bought a gun, and he'd made sure he did it at work, not at her place. Being a journalist quickly wised you up on a thousand silly ways to die.

He'd had no doubt that sooner or later Chloe Melville was going to shoot him in 'self defense,' and that afterwards she'd not understand why she'd done it, and even the twenty or thirty years of padded-cell psychoanalysis the state of Massachusetts would prescribe for her wouldn't help her understanding much.

***

And so they rolled south through the town. Soon they hit this Raynham's version of the New State Highway (aka Massachusetts Route 44), complete with its twin expanses of flanking shopping malls. A few shoppers were in evidence. Just a regular lazy Sunday morning.

Nick silently wondered if they had any churches here, and if they did, what their denominations might be. Though he only went to church during family weddings and funerals, he found it an intriguing question; something to ponder while Todd followed Seer Jonah and Drake's two women.

Traffic was sparse; Sunday morning again. They continued along the New State Highway, stopping at another traffic light. The light hadn't caught Melody's brown SUV, and so she'd parked on the other side of the intersection to wait for them.

Fifty yards down the road from the traffic light, they could see the red and yellow signboard for a McDonald's eatery.

"Where the hell is this crazy guy taking us?" Todd grunted angrily, taking his hand off the wheel to scratch his cheek.

Nick didn't reply. Remembering that Todd's handgun was lying in plain view on his lap, he tensed as a cop on a motorbike rode past.

Actually, the weirdest thing of all today, was that so far Todd hadn't lit a single cigarette. Normally Todd would be chain-smoking.

Which just goes to show how flustered he is beneath that tough exterior, Nick thought in some amusement. *But really, I can't blame the guy.*

Chloe pointed out of her window at a T-Mobile shop. "So what you're saying now is, that we can drive over there and sign up for T-Mobile, only it won't be our T-Mobile we're gonna get, but this world's version? Guys, just the thought of it makes my head hurt. Hey, and you know what's *really* weird about all this? Well, right now I feel like I ought to be scared shitless, but everything looks so much the same as I remember—so frigging everyday northeast USA—that I don't see anything to be scared of. Even the damn sky just looks like evening, or early morning in midwinter after there's been a heavy fall of snow overnight."

Nick agreed with her. The traffic lights changed from red to green and Todd put their car in motion again.

While watching the shops go past, Nick thought, *Yeah, Chloe's right. At the moment I should be scared poopless too. The problem is that I don't see anything to be scared of.*

CHAPTER 14

Chloe

Though doing her best to capture her on-the-spot impressions of the town they were driving through, Chloe's thoughts kept drifting.

This strangeness that wasn't so strange was just too strange.

She'd been trying to ignore the divergences from what she was used to, thinking that such an attitude would better help her cope with this place.

Well, according to Seer Jonah, and from what I've seen so far, there really is very little difference. Okay, actually we don't have flying people back home . . .

So, Chloe recorded what she saw and felt about this place. To save time and work faster, she used her own personal shorthand, using keywords that she would later expand into passages of journalistic prose to stimulate the minds of her readers.

To an extent she disagreed with Todd's statement that the US government was certain to muzzle any attempt of theirs to break the news about this place. She was a journalist, for God's sake. Naively or not, she honestly viewed telling the truth as her life's calling and had made lots of sacrifices to be where she was today; because she wanted to be recognized as one of the best in her field. She wanted to be lauded and applauded; she wanted to win awards. The Pulitzer Prize wasn't just for others.

And now it looks like my time has come, as in REALLY come. At last all the pain will be worth it.

With a feeling of great sadness in her heart, Chloe thought back on the greatest of the sacrifices she'd made for the sake of her journalistic career. And yes, back then even Drake had advised against the decision she'd taken, saying she was being silly by doing so.

***

Eight years ago.

23-year-old Chloe Melville had just begun working at the Boston Globe. Back home in Ohio for the weekend, that fateful Saturday night she'd accompanied Drake to the birthday party of one of his ex-girlfriends who lived over in Springfield. At that point in time Drake's meeting and romancing (and later marrying) Elizabeth Mary Turner still lay two months in the future.

Anyway, they'd attended the party together.

At first Chloe had had a blast, meeting new people and catching up on old times with the birthday girl Tessa Lau, whom she knew well from college. Tessa Lau was Chinese and a fun person to be around, with what was best described as a 'gummy' smile.

But then things had turned nasty for Chloe. At some point in the evening, someone must have slipped a drug into her drink.

Chloe's next recollections were hazy. All she remembered of the next three hours was lying in a bed while several warm and naked bodies pressed on hers. And entered hers. She'd instantly begun hurting between her legs; something was rubbing inside her that didn't feel right; literally rubbing her the wrong way; but she was too out of it to tell them to stop.

She'd felt as if she was dreaming, because the faces of the people with her were all blurred out like pencil drawings smudged with an eraser. Similarly, everyone's voices formed a musical blend like a demonic masculine choir, that is, when they weren't grunting or laughing, which inserted several psychotically funny if dislocated interludes into her confused daze. At several points something warm and throbbing had been inserted in her mouth and she'd sucked and chewed apathetically on it.

And the hurting between her legs had continued. She'd been too exhausted, it seemed, to push the pain away; too tired to protest; too weakened to do anything else but lie on her back, or on her belly when she was rolled over and twisted and contorted into strange positions again and again, as if those manipulating her limp form couldn't make up their minds on what to do with it. At one point she was lifted off the bed and suspended in midair, with lots of hard and painful things entering her one after the other while she felt like crying and everyone else laughed.

Finally the warm and naked people had left her and she'd slept.

Next thing Chloe knew, Drake was shaking her awake. He was both concerned and mad. This was when she realized that she'd been slipped a date-rape drug, and on the pretext that she'd merely drunk too much and needed to sleep it off, had been carried up into Tessa's guest bedroom and fucked by whoever wanted her.

Drake had suggested calling the cops. Tessa Lau had seconded this.

Tessa was distraught that something like this had happened in her house; and on her birthday, for that matter. Her concern for Chloe's wellbeing had leeched her of both comeliness and vitality, leaving her shrunken, almost a gnome sitting at the foot of the bed. Combined with the sense of dislocation caused by the receding rape drug in her blood stream, the young Chinese hostess's wavy brown-and-pink hair, slight stature, and very thick eyebrows had made her seem alien to Chloe, a visitor to the planet.

"Oh my God, I'll never forgive myself for letting this happen to you," she'd said, with tears flooding her dark eyes. "I had absolutely no idea that anything bad was going on in here. I thought you were fast asleep."

Chloe, however, had refused to let them persuade her to call the police.

"It's too early in my career to stigmatize myself," she'd protested against their own protests.

"But . . . you mean, you're just gonna let them get away with it?" Drake had asked angrily. He'd been so enraged, that even though she and not he was the victim, she'd been glad that Tessa didn't have a gun at home. Drake had seemed mad enough to shoot any number of people involved in her defilement.

"I agree with him one hundred percent," Tessa Lau had said, scratching nervously at a little mole on the right side of her upper lip. "We need to get the cops over here fast and let them do a rape kit for you."

Chloe had pulled up the covers over her breasts and shook her head vigorously. "So what? So that I can be labelled the 'Girl Who Cried Rape?' Sorry, guys, but I don't want the notoriety. Like I said, in addition to making me a joke among my colleagues, who'll of course all pretend they sympathize with my suffering, this is very likely to mess up my career big-time. Whenever I'll be mentioned afterwards, I'll always be notable for the wrong reason."

Before they could say any more, Chloe had leapt off the bed and run into Tessa's bathroom, where she'd locked the door and turned on the shower.

Thinking she planned on hurting herself in there, Drake and Tessa Lau began banging on the door. "Hey, open up! Open up!"

She'd heard Drake asking Tessa if she kept any razors in there. Then, realizing that the two of them might call the police anyway if they thought she was committing suicide in the bathroom, she finally opened the door and let them in; but then immediately stepped back under the shower and began soaping herself vigorously between her legs again.

Shit! It hurt like hell down there, both front and back, but she made a bold show of biting back on her agony and not letting her brother and his friend see how much pain she was in.

"What are you doing?" Drake asked angrily.

"What does it look like I'm doing, big brother?" she'd replied him, matching the anger on his face. "I'm washing away all the DNA evidence. Like I said, my career as a journalist has just begun and I don't need any gangbang shit sullying my reputation. Maybe I'll do a *Me Too* on those guys later, when I'm famous. But not now. Hell no, not yet."

Her abusers had used condoms, so she hadn't caught any STIs; but at least one of them had fucked her roughly in the ass—afterwards she'd shit blood for three days. Her rectal bleeding had only cleared up on the morning she'd planned to see her doctor about it.

***

Did I make the right choice back then? Chloe wondered now as she remembered. *Oh, maybe I should have listened to Drake and Tessa and let the cops investigate and prosecute the rapists. The damn reporting career I was so desperate to protect hasn't exactly been a raging success so far. Who knows? The notoriety of having been raped might even have made me famous back then. It isn't like I'm the only woman it's ever happened to. Lots of women suffer the same fate and they do talk about it, do get justice for themselves. They survive.*

But did she really regret her decision? She didn't know. She knew she hadn't wanted pity and sympathy back then; she'd just wanted to get on with her life on her own terms, to face her bright future as if nothing bad had happened in that bedroom that evening.

But of course, that had proved impossible.

Chloe's rape experience had totally messed up her sex life. Each time she dated a man, she kept thinking he was about slipping a Mickey Finn into her drinks so he could have his nasty way with her while she was unconscious. It made her mad enough to kill the guy. And the sex? Nowadays sex made her feel powerless, like she had no control over her destiny. Even when she had multiple orgasms she hated herself, hated her body's betrayal of her. She couldn't shake the feeling that she'd been raped because she was weak; that if she'd been stronger, nothing would have happened to her. Drake had tried to talk her through this, but nothing he'd said had made the slightest difference. Like she'd bluntly told him: "I'm the one hurting, not you; so leave me to deal with this my own way."

"Your way is taking forever," he'd kindly pointed out. "And all you're doing is hurting yourself even more. Little sis, I think it's best if you see a shrink."

She'd seen a therapist in the past. And since breaking up with Nick—and yes, many times she *had* felt like shooting him after they made love, even though it had been with her consent and he'd made her come—was currently seeing another shrink twice a week.

She hated the rapists now; hated how they'd ruined her. She'd hated them back then too. All she wanted now was a normal life, a normal sex life with a loving man, and to put those nauseating and horrible memories behind her.

But would she ever get what she wanted?

***

"Will someone please tell me why we're slowing down now?" Todd was grumbling angrily when Chloe resurfaced from her miserable trip down memory lane.

The brown BMW SUV they were following was turning into the parking lot of the McDonald's that they'd glimpsed from the traffic lights.

"I dunno. Maybe Seer Jonah's hungry again," Nick joked.

Todd turned in after the SUV. "I swear to God Almighty that I'll shoot that asshole if he's jerking us around."

"Calm down, man," Chloe said soothingly from the backseat. "Look, the others are all getting out. I think Drake is in there."

Todd grimaced. "What? He works here now flipping burgers?"

Dude, you really, really frigging need to calm yourself, Chloe thought while Todd parked next to the SUV.

Then they got out and joined the others.

CHAPTER 15

Liz

The McDonald's restaurant was mostly empty. Its sole occupant besides Drake was the female angelus tending the counter.

Liz and Melody were first into the building, stepping up past a sign saying the place was 'closed till tomorrow for maintenance work.' Chloe and her journalist crew were getting their gear out of their car, while Seer Jonah was also explaining something about the neighborhood to Nick.

Now that they were here, Liz felt small and vulnerable.

As she stepped into the building she eyed the winged woman behind the counter with dread, taking care to keep as far away from her she could. She couldn't shake her fear that this female was a dangerous beast that could attack her without just cause.

The angelus was about her own height—5 feet 4 inches tall—and was wearing a McDonald's staff uniform. Well, sort of. She had on black-and-gray pants, black sneakers, and a black baseball cap with twin yellow arches on it. But instead of a shirt, she wore a gray halter top, clearly because of her wings.

Her hair was brown and cropped short, possibly so as not to get tangled in her wings, which were large, had brown feathers and were folded neatly on her back with their tips reaching down to her thighs. Her skin was pale and her eyes a deep green. She seemed to be of Asian extraction.

She smiled at the two women, revealing normal teeth, and gestured into the dining hall with both hands. "Welcome, and please come in. Mr. Drake has been expecting you all." Her English sounded American enough.

Glad to get even further away from the angelus, Liz followed the impatient Melody as she strode briskly past the rows of unoccupied formica-topped tables towards the famous man waiting in the middle of the dining hall.

Drake was already getting up to welcome them.

"Honey!" Melody hollered and ran away from Liz and into her husband's arms, which were outstretched to receive her. And then the pair were kissing one another passionately and Melody was crying, while Drake stroked her hair and petted her.

Liz held back from walking over there to join them; she let the reunited couple have their family space.

She was both shocked and amused when all of a sudden, clearly in the grip of an emotional impulse, Melody stepped back from her husband and smacked him hard in the face.

Drake reeled back in shock. Anger instantly flashed across his face, but was just as quickly followed by confusion.

"What did you do that for?!" he asked.

"How dare you abandon me like that!?" Melody yelled at him, and next leapt at him again, this time to resume kissing him, while Drake held her close again, and waved at Liz behind her back.

"Hi there, glad you could make it," he greeted her airily.

"Wasn't like you gave me much choice," she replied in some anger. "Not considering the creepy way you summoned me. How could you do that to your own son?"

She figured Drake would have replied her, but Melody, seeming to grow angry that she wasn't the entire focus of her husband's attention, once more lifted her mouth to his and began kissing him.

Watching the happy and emotional reunion between Drake and his wife, Liz couldn't help but feel jealous. It had literally been ages since she'd seem similar desire for herself in a man's eyes.

She sighed. *Well that chapter's over now. At least we had some good fun last night. That's our secret; Melody promised she wouldn't tell Drake about it.* But looking at the love shining from the transsexual woman eyes, Liz knew that pledge wasn't worth the kiss that had sealed it. Sooner or later— most likely after having her ass fucked hard like she'd been craving for the past three years—Melody Melville was certain to spill the beans on what they'd done last night.

But well, I guess it doesn't really matter, does it, if we both share the same woman. Then Liz felt lonely, deserted. *Ah, how I wish Bonnie were here now.*

She also wished for a working phone network to call her father and son.

But yes, I know that's just wishful thinking—we're completely cut off from our own world. But if we are, how then was Drake able to send texts to Chloe and Melody? But even if that's possible, I'd still need to be subscribed to a network here; or maybe I can simply borrow Drake's phone later? She shrugged at the possibilities. *Best of all, let's just get this family reunion over with quickly and I'll see dad and Frankie soon enough. Though from the look of things, Melody is gonna be hanging around here for a while.*

She heard noises behind her and turned back towards the door of the dining hall.

Seer Jonah and the journalists were just coming in, with the angelus following after them. The winged woman was holding a small notepad.

Chloe in the lead, the others soon arrived at Drake's table, with Liz stepping aside to let them pass.

For Liz, the novelty of seeing Drake again after all this while was already wearing off. Once more she felt suspicious of him and wondered why he'd asked her to accompany Melody here. Was it just that he wanted to speak to her about their son, or did he have an ulterior motive? It had just occurred to Liz that if Drake killed her here—here in this world that no one suspected existed—he could easily get away with the murder.

Melody was still sobbing with joy as she tightly hugged her husband.

Wow, she's pressed up so tight against him, she looks like she's rubbing a hard-on against his leg, like to really show him how much she's missed him.

Anyway, Melody showed no sign of letting go of Drake, so Chloe had to be satisfied with a handshake and a peck on the cheek as her own greeting on being reunited with her long-lost brother.

Oops. What if I've gotten pregnant for Melody? The sudden thought at once horrified and amused Liz intensely. She'd been so sexually aroused last night that she'd completely forgotten about contraception. Social diseases might be a concern too. *But Melody clearly hasn't been sleeping around, so there's nothing to worry about there. And I'm clean too, so it ain't like I've given her anything either. But—fuck—pregnancy is a definite possibility with all that come she pumped into me. Assuming I am knocked up, should I terminate the pregnancy or keep the child?* She smirked. *Keeping it might be kinda fun. If nothing else, it'll create a really weird family dynamic—me having borne kids for both my ex-husband and his wife.*

Then Chloe introduced everyone, and after the hellos were all completed, Seer Jonah and the angelus (who was named Jade) pushed two restaurant tables together and everyone sat around them. The exception to this was Todd, who remained standing with his video camera to film their gathering. Drake was sandwiched between Nick and Melody. Chloe, who expected to conduct an interview, sat directly facing her brother, with Liz on her left hand and Seer Jonah on her right.

Drake still looked how Liz remembered him; the man she'd both loved and detested in equal measure: handsome and of average height, with smiling brown eyes and cornsilk hair. A pea from the same blond pod as his delighted sister. He was dressed in a black S.U.A.F.M tee shirt, faded blue jeans and black sneakers. Thirty-five years old now, but yes, he looked older; and maybe a little bit overworked too. He seemed more wiry; a little shriveled even.

"Yes, you're all welcome here," Drake said once everyone except Todd and Jade were seated. "And, oh yes, I know everyone has lots of questions for me, and I'll answer everyone's queries in due course. But first, would anyone like some coffee . . . or something else to drink . . . or even to eat, perhaps? Although I expect that as instructed, Seer Jonah already prepared a hearty breakfast for you all?"

He made a gesture towards the angelus, who was placing a potted plant near the middle of the joined tables. "Jade, please take their orders."

The winged woman made a final adjustment to her potted plant and then stepped back, pulling out her notepad from a trouser pocket as she did so. "So, yes, what can I get you all?" she enquired.

Liz felt nonplussed by everything.

"A coffee for me; cappuccino if you've got it," Melody instantly ordered, then once more pressed up closely against Drake. She seemed to be finding it impossible to let go of him. And Liz was now certain that, yes, her lover of last night did indeed have an erection and was doing her best to hide it in her hot pants. She'd earlier told Liz that the hot pants were intended to give Drake an eyeful of what he'd been missing for the past three years.

Staring at the angelus though, beautiful and enigmatic as she was, and both alien and human at the same time, Liz wondered if her ex had really missed his current wife all that much.

But he seems just as delighted to see her as she is to see him, she thought with jealousy. Then she realized that Jade was staring at her, her leaf-green eyes as piercing as Chinese arrows. Her gaze was bothersome, as sharp as a knife peeling away a person's skin.

Now why the hell did I just think that?

"I'll just have a Pepsi, thanks," she told the strange woman. And then, more pleasantly, Jade's green eyes reminded her of the plant she'd earlier placed on the table, so when the angelus turned to take Chloe's order, Liz studied that potted plant.

She saw that it was actually a miniature tree, like a Japanese bonsai tree. The tree gave off a heavy fragrance—like a mixture of jasmine and orange zest—which perhaps explained why it had been placed on the table: to function as an air freshener. Amusingly, this pungent little tree was as withered as its larger cousins outside the McDonald's, which observation made Liz glance out of the wide windows opposite her to study the sparse Sunday morning traffic traversing the highway.

Once Jade had taken all their orders and left, Drake resumed speaking:

"Well, first of all, I must announce to you all, and I'm obviously saying this mainly for the benefit of the press folks present—meaning my darling sister and Nick and Todd, so they can capture this moment on film for posterity's sake—yes, I have indeed finished writing my new book. Yes, ladies and gents, my magnum opus *The Book of Atrocities* is finished. It's a reality. My publishers will of course be delighted to once more give the planet nightmares, and," he added, waving a finger in the air for emphasis, "this one'll make me another pretty packet of money too."

There was laughter around the table, even from the tough and cynical Todd Wilson, whom, now that he'd realized Seer Jonah hadn't tricked them after all, had finally lit up his first cigarette of the day.

"Oh, once this new book is published, I'll have the world at my feet," Drake said with a broad smile. "And I mean that literally, not in a literary sense." He burst out laughing.

"Oh, I'm sure you will, darling," Melody commented dryly with an indulgent smile, while Liz wondered where he'd suddenly gotten this streak of megalomania from. *The world at his feet? Drake, it's just another novel! Hundreds of bestsellers get published each year. It ain't like the publishing industry quit working in your absence.*

"Yes," Drake repeated, as if he could read her doubts on her face, or maybe to ensure no one missed his point. "Once my *Book of Atrocities* hits bookstores worldwide, I'll literally have the world at my feet!"

Liz felt a deep unease at his words, but she figured this was his moment of glory, so why not, right?

***

Liz was amused by Drake's tee shirt. The shirt was promo for superstar rock band Slain Jane's S.U.A.F.M (or 'Shut Up and Fuck Me') album. She wondered if Melody got the ironic reference to Drake's last girlfriend before he'd met her. But snuggled up against her husband's chest like she was now, Melody seemed too blissed-out with reunion ecstasy to even have noticed the shirt at all.

That might come later. It's weird though—like Drake's surrounding himself today with all the women he's ever loved. But no, he told me he couldn't love Jane!

Oh, that had been weird. Slain Jane's lead singer Janet Orgasm had entered Drake's life shortly after *The Bleeding Oysters* had been published. Drake was on his way up, up, up and Slain Jane were at the top of their game, the band then enjoying a No. 1 Billboard hit with the ballad *Blood Sisters*. The pair been an item for about six months, with the paparazzi making bets on when they'd get married; the scandalous writer and the trashy and regularly wasted rock star. Slain Jane's new S.U.A.F.M album had even contained several songs based on Drake's hit novel.

But then the couple had had a fight and gone their separate ways.

Liz giggled. Reasons given for the breakup? One tabloid report said Jane had gotten mad when Drake drunkenly pissed on her dog Lupus. Another version said that after catching Drake kissing a female fan, Jane had brewed rat droppings as coffee for him, giving him severe food poisoning.

Liz yawned. There had been loads of crazy stories about the couple. Maybe none of them were true. Maybe all of them were. Liz had met Janet Orgasm in person once. The crazy bitch had more than lived up to all the scandal and hype about her . . . and then some.

But hey, Liz remembered now, turning to staring worriedly back across the dining hall at Jade, who was just stepping out from behind the wide McDonald's counter with a laden tray of drinks, *wasn't there one more rumor about Drake and Jane's breakup? Something about her claiming she'd walked into a room in his house and met an angel in there . . . a FEMALE angel who'd then tried to kill her? But of course, no one believed Jane. Everyone just assumed she'd been more stoned out of her mind than usual!*

***

"It's great to see you again," Chloe enthused. She got up, leaned over the table and clipped a microphone to Drake's chest, then took her seat again. After nodding enquiringly at Todd, who was standing by the left end of the table, and who replied with a thumbs up, she said: "Alright, rich and famous older brother, if you don't mind a few questions from the press, let's get down to business. According to Seer Jonah, we need to hurry before the portal closes, or we might be stuck here for a while and my cat'll start missing me."

"Fire away," Drake said good-humoredly.

Chloe beamed. "Alright then. So, this place, this strange alternate *Static Earth* realm, how did you discover it in the first place?"

"Oh, it discovered me, really," Drake replied. "And largely by accident at that." He glanced over at Liz. "My lovely ex here might recall all those times when there seemed to be invisible people in our home." He winked at her. "That female voice you once heard, I mean that time when the additional wineglass was on our coffee table at midnight . . . well, that was Jade."

Liz gasped. "What? Oh, you were cheating on me with her?"

Drake laughed. "Oh no. Back then, we'd just met. Though Jade is clearly a lovely creature, I was too scared to touch her." He shrugged. "The sex came later; after you and I got divorced, and I was lonely. She comforted me then."

Melody pushed him away and frowned at him. "Oh, so you did screw her later? And how about now? Are you still sleeping with that winged bitch?"

He shook his head. "Darling, it was just a fling—might even have been love for a while, but it's over now. Was over long before I met you, in fact."

Melody still looked pissed off. Liz covered her mouth with her hand to hide her amusement. *Poor girl. She's probably thinking of all the dick she could have sucked and ridden in his absence if she'd only known he was banging Jade over here.*

But oddly, Drake seemed pained by Melody's accusation of infidelity. "Honey," he said, "if I've got a girlfriend here, why the hell would I ask *you* to come over? All that would do is screw things up, right? And . . . and didn't I continue to look after you in my absence? That shows I never stopped caring about you, don't it?"

Melody mused on that for a while, then she giggled. "Oh alright, baby. I guess what's done is done. But I'm warning you: if I catch her looking at you seductively, I'll cut her wings off!"

"Whose wings are you gonna cut off, honey?" Jade asked quietly, arriving as if on cue with their tray of beverages. Liz, who was seated with her back to the McDonald's counter, had no idea how much of Melody's bitching the angelus had overheard, but the winged woman now had a scowl on her face and her brown wings seemed higher up on her back than before, like those of a bird preparing to take flight; as if she was barely restraining herself from unfurling them and leaping over the table to beat up Melody Melville.

"Oh, never mind, darling," Melody chirped quickly. "Thanks for the coffee!"

Laughter around the table. Jade handing everyone their drinks. Todd recording everything.

Liz, who as an actress, was very familiar with television studios' editing practices, wondered how much of this footage of Drake the networks would dare use.

It isn't like this is normal footage. But then she questioned herself: *Alright, but what's abnormal about it? We're in a McDonald's, for crying out loud! The most American of eateries. Every American town worth its name has at least one of those. Only reason this place isn't full of folks now is 'cos of that sign outside that says they're closed for maintenance today. And outside, there's a highway with Fords and Chevrolets and Toyotas and Hondas and—never forget the trucks—lots of GMC and Ford pickups rolling past. Who the hell is ever gonna believe that we filmed this on another version of the planet? I mean, I find it hard to believe I'm someplace else and I'm right here. About the most exciting thing that's so far happened here is Drake and Melody's argument; and the pair of them have already made up again, with Melody once more looking like she wants to rip off his pants already and start riding him.*

She sighed. *So, honey pie me, the networks don't even have to say they filmed Drake anywhere else—they can use this footage as it is and no one will ever know the difference. Oh yeah, I forgot: there's a winged woman serving us coffee. Yeah, you don't see winged women working in regular McDonald's restaurants. But who's gonna believe she isn't special effects? Oh, and I forgot Seer Jonah.*

She was surprised that she'd forgotten the tattooed man, but then realized it was because he'd been completely silent since they'd entered the McDonald's. She looked around the tables for him. He was seated on her far right, next to Chloe, and was busy cleaning his fingernails with a toothpick.

Across the table, Nick, who was seated on Drake's right and was thus directly opposite her, caught her eye between sips of his coffee and faked a yawn. She laughed back, and yawned too and sipped her Pepsi, hoping its caffeine content would boost her; the ordinariness of this place was making her sleepy.

"I'd suggest you refrain from making remarks like that about Jade, honey," Drake suddenly told Melody. "She already doesn't like you very much."

Melody, however, merely glanced dismissively at the angelus, as if this revelation had reduced the winged woman to the importance of a fried McDonald's chicken in her eyes, then she scowled back at Drake. "Doesn't like me? Why? I don't even know her—like, we're from different planets?"

"Well, darling," Drake explained, "it's because she's in love with me, and you're the only reason I can't marry her. See, I told Jade that I love *you*, and wouldn't look at another woman while you're still alive."

Oh that's rather cruel of him, Liz thought, with a sudden burst of sympathy for Melody. *He really shouldn't have said that in front of her.* But then she became confused: which woman was Drake being more cruel to by making this statement? Was it Melody, who was learning for the first time of her romantic rival? Or the winged Jade, who was having her privately expressed feelings for him publicly revealed for all present to hear. Not to mention that Todd was recording all of this for the public back home to watch. *If I was Jade, I'd be completely mortified!*

But Jade didn't seem to mind. She was actually smiling coldly at Melody. "Yes, darling, I do love him," she even admitted, her lips parting seductively. "And yes, we were lovers once. But that was years ago. Now your husband is completely faithful to you. He told me that so long as you were *alive* he'd never so much as glance at another woman."

Jade had placed unmistakable emphasis on the word 'alive' and Melody finally got what she meant. Her face paled and she turned to Drake. "Oh, darling, you don't think she'd . . . ?"

He grinned and stroked her black hair. "All I'm saying is—don't piss the woman off. Beautiful as Jade is, I'm not yet looking to marry wife number three."

Melody gulped and nodded. Jade smiled coolly at her and walked over to sit next to Seer Jonah. She began whispering something to Seer Jonah that made him laugh.

Liz yawned again. *Okay, so their little domestic dispute's once more been resolved. Hey, can we get down to serious matters now?*

Chloe had seemed alarmed at the conflict between Drake and Melody. Now she reset her calm interviewer's smile, smoothed her blonde hair and said, "Okay, so let's continue our interview, shall we? . . . So, alright, Drake, at what point did it occur to you to . . . ?" Chloe stopped speaking and yawned so wide that Liz could see her tonsils. It was amazing really; she was so tired she didn't even cover her mouth.

Liz wondered why she and Chloe were both yawning. *Is it something in our drinks? But I'm drinking Pepsi and she's got a Coke. Both of those are loaded with caffeine.*

And then, sensing something odd going on behind her, Liz spun towards Todd. And without warning, Todd suddenly slumped forward. Liz watched it happen, like in a dream.

First Todd yawned too. Then his eyes glazed over and his body slackened. Then he keeled forward, slowly, while trying to prevent the expensive video camera from falling. He managed to slide the camera down the tabletop towards everyone, and then next thing, he hit the table face-first. His eyes shut, his mouth fell open, and his cigarette shot from his lips and rolled off the side of the table.

It only took Liz one look to tell that Todd was out cold. She yawned herself and tried to figure out what had just happened to him.

But, dear God, she felt so damn tired.

Then she realized that the others were yawning too.

Hey, what's going on here?

Nick's head fell and hit the table. It was very sudden; from sitting upright and trying to focus his eyes on the cup of coffee in his hand, the next moment his head dropped and the coffee cup went flying through the air, spilling its contents all over Todd, who clearly didn't even notice he'd been splattered.

Chloe fell asleep next, slipping sideways half out of her chair, with her head finally banging against Liz's shoulder.

Confused, Liz looked at the others. But then she mistakenly yawned in the direction of the potted plant that Jade had placed on the table. Immediately she drew in that breath of air, she felt twice as tired. Now she could hardly keep her eyes open.

Still she managed to raise her head and stare at her ex. Drake was smiling coldly; he didn't look sleepy at all. Melody was slumped against his chest though; already passed out. Drake nodded down the table at Jade and Seer Jonah, who both got to their feet and approached the sleeping people.

It's the damn plant that's putting us all to sleep. It's a trick! Drake's tricked us. I need to remain awake!

But her head was already dropping towards the tabletop and she was out cold—far into dreamland—before the table smacked her in the face.

CHAPTER 16

Chloe

Hey, what just happened back there?

This was Chloe's first thought on opening her eyes. *What on earth happened to me?*

Then she realized she was no longer sitting opposite Drake in the McDonald's restaurant. Alarm hit her like a bullet.

Oh my God!

She and the others—everyone who'd been in the McDonald's—were now in some kind of large chamber.

She and Nick were tied to steel chairs. Both chairs were securely bolted to the floor. Todd was seated in another bolted-in-place chair on her left and was busy attaching his video camera to its tripod. Liz and Melody Melville were both bound to the wall opposite Nick and herself.

Drake, Seer Jonah and the angelus Jade were standing beside a large black curtain that obscured the room's right wall. The trio of kidnappers were talking animatedly, but in hushed voices.

The same perplexed question replayed through Chloe's mind again: *What the hell is going on here? Okay, I get it that we were drugged somehow. But what the hell is Drake up to?*

The two wives weren't saying anything; or if they were they were whispering to themselves. Anyhow, Chloe couldn't see their faces. Both of them had been stripped completely naked and arranged facing the wall, with their bodies touching and their hands apparently bound in front of them, their ankles also secured with ropes.

Strangest of all was the weird writing across their backs. Chloe quickly realized that it was similar to the ancient script tattooed across Seer Jonah's body. The way the words were written was very unusual: the sentences were clearly written 'across' both women's bodies, with some words even split in two—the first half on Liz, the remaining syllables on Melody (and with the script then carrying on until it reached her right side), then the next line began on Liz's left side—as if both of their backs together formed a single sheet of paper.

Of Chloe own companions, Nick was still asleep on her right and Todd was intent on getting his camera set up, so she, always the reporter, looked around to see what else was in here.

She quickly deduced that this chamber was a storeroom, maybe one even located in the rear of that same McDonald's restaurant.

There were two giant walk-in freezers behind her and this place was also full of metal racks loaded up with boxes and miscellaneous tools. The room's corners were piled high with large cartons. In addition to this, several lockers labeled with people's names stood on her left, behind Todd.

The room had no windows. Which made sense: would a kidnapper hide those he'd abducted in view of passersby?

The room's smell of blood and meat worried her. Not as much as being kidnapped did, however. The freezers behind her must contain meat; that was logical enough. What wasn't logical though, was why Drake (who'd always loved her and treated her like a princess) had tied her up. She felt like yelling at him to untie her, but then felt a fear of doing so; there was something very sinister about the way he, Seer Jonah and Jade were whispering that made her think twice about letting them know she'd awoken.

She'd quickly understood that this setup Drake had here wasn't something random, thrown together on the spur of the moment.

Oh, he's been planning this for a long while!

She looked over at Liz and Melody, who were both shaking their heads as if groggy. Mouths gagged with duct tape, they tried looking over their shoulders; their eyes pleading for help.

They're the reason for this! Once more Chloe's eyes took in the strange inscriptions across the two women's backs. Oh, she had no doubt that her brother had lured them both here for some reason.

But what can that reason possibly be? He wants to 'punish' his wives? No, that's too crazy to even consider. But what? Why?

One thing was certain. Chloe felt in no personal danger. Drake would never hurt her. He loved her. He'd demonstrated that affection over and over through the years since they'd been kids. When she'd been raped he'd been her backbone. She'd never told their parents anything. Drake had been the one who'd kept her strong then and helped her carry on with her life. He'd always supported her decisions, always watched out for her.

So Chloe knew she was safe; just as she knew too that the only reason she and Nick were tied up was because Drake didn't want them interfering in what he wanted to do to his wives. Todd was free, but that was easy to understand: Drake wanted documented proof of his crime, whatever that crime would be.

But though Chloe loved her older brother, she also loved fair play and justice. She couldn't just sit back and watch him hurt her ex- and current sisters-in-law.

Her hands were tied behind the chair. She tried to work them free but failed. Her fingers couldn't quite reach the knots in the ropes. So instead she looked at Todd again.

The ex-marine had finished setting up his video camera now and was lighting up a cigarette. He noticed her staring at him and shushed her before she could speak. He pointed down at his left ankle, which she now saw was cuffed to the sturdy chair he was sitting on, and then whispered: "That asshole Seer took my gun. That's it over there, on the ground next to Nick."

Chloe turned quickly and saw the Glock on the floor, about a yard from Nick's feet.

She looked up and her eyes met with Seer Jonah's. He smiled at her and she shuddered. *How the hell didn't I realize how evil that man is? He's likely the one who talked Drake into all this.* A brief replay of all the atrocities the man had committed in *The Bleeding Oysters* ran though her mind and now she felt real fear: *What if he's convinced Drake to hurt me too? But for the moment that seems unlikely. I'm still dressed and just tied up. Melody and Liz are the ones they wanted.*

Seer Jonah returned his attention to his conversation with her brother and she turned back to look worriedly at Todd. "How do we stop this? What do we do?"

"We play it by ear," he whispered back. "Just follow my lead, and we'll stop whatever your crazy bro is out to do to those two ladies." He frowned. "Seer Jonah drew that nonsense on their backs—like he was writing in a book or something. They both woke up screaming, but the asshole punched them both in the back of the head and knocked them out again. I swear to God, once I get my hands on him, I'll teach him to treat women better than that."

Chloe nodded. "Any idea how they doped us?"

"Has to be something they put in our drinks, though my coffee didn't taste—"

"Well, well, well, my darling sister's awake!" Drake interrupted him, his voice loud and cheerful. "So now, let's get on with it, shall we?"

"What are you up to, Drake? Why've you got me tied up like this?" Chloe asked, trying to make her voice sound tough. She was very aware of Jade smirking at her and didn't want to give her the satisfaction of seeing how scared she now was. Nor Seer Jonah either, who'd walked across to Liz and Melody and was studying the black writing on their backs.

"Should I take the duct tape off their mouths?" Seer Jonah asked.

"Not yet," Drake told him. "It's best they don't start screaming again or we'll never hear the last of it. But please, Seer, do turn them both around to face me."

As Seer Jonah hurried to comply with Drake's request, Chloe saw that in addition to having both their wrists and ankles bound, two ropes also ran from Melody's and Liz's wrists to a metal ring set in the wall at about waist height. These twin ropes looped through this hoop and then ran upward to a hook above the two women's heads, from which the unused ends of both ropes dangled. The logic behind this setup seemed to be that her brother could easily either lengthen or shorten the amount of rope between his captives and the wall, and by so doing permit them varying degrees of movement.

Initially, both women's hands had been secured right next to the wall, which was why they'd been unable to turn around. But now, once Seer Jonah paid out more rope from the overhead hook, Liz and Melody were both able to turn and face the others in the storeroom.

Okay, so that was that. However, Chloe wondered how Drake intended to prevent Liz and Melody from removing their gags of duct-tape by themselves now that their hands were freer.

But a simple threat sufficed to deter them from attempting to do so.

"Alright," Seer Jonah told them coldly. "If either of you bitches dare take off your gags, I'll cut out your tongues and make you eat them, okay?"

Chloe had no idea what else (in addition to punching them in the head like Todd had told her) Seer Jonah had done to Melody and Liz while she'd been unconscious, but he must have scared them immensely, because both women immediately nodded and stood there passively, completely cowed. Even from across the room, Chloe could read it in their eyes that they totally believed he'd do what he'd just threatened. It was sickening to see how scared of him they were; and it made her mad at both her brother and this tattooed henchman of his.

Once certain that both frightened women were paying attention to him, Drake pointed at Nick. "Now, Seer, wake *him* up. I expect him to survive this, so he might as well know what it's all about."

The tattooed man nodded, and leaving the two bound women mumbling piteous entreaties, crossed the room towards Chloe. Jade took his place beside the two women, momentarily spreading her wings and creating a breeze in the storeroom. Melody, her mascara running in thick lines down her face, looked like she was going to faint the closer Jade stepped to her. And it seemed the angelus knew Melody was terrified of her and wanted to taunt her further still. She had a cruel smile on her pretty face and only desisted in tormenting the bound women when Drake shook his head at her. Then she frowned at him and began pouting.

"Don't you dare hurt him!" Chloe told Seer Jonah as he leaned over Nick.

"Don't worry, miss, I won't," Seer Jonah replied her. "I only hurt people I wish to save. And your brother hasn't marked Mr. Sinclair for salvation today."

He pinched Nick's nose shut and covered his mouth with his other hand. Then he waited. It took about thirty seconds for Nick to begin struggling to breathe. Then he snapped awake sputtering.

"What the . . . ? Hey, you dickhead . . . why am I tied up like this?" He glared angrily up at Seer Jonah. "Hey, untie me! As in, right now. C'mon do it!"

Drake walked over and stared down at Nick. "Thanks for finally joining us, Mr. Sinclair. And I would advise you to calm down and hear what I've got to tell you all. This is a historic moment for both of our worlds"—he looked at Seer Jonah and Jade and they smiled conspiratorially—"so please just calm down and listen, and make sure you properly understand what I'm about to do here."

Chloe thought Nick looked enraged enough to develop superpowers and burst through his bonds and out of his chair, but then he simmered down and just looked pissed off. "Okay, shoot, I'm listening," he said. "And then frigging untie us all. I don't appreciate this bondage crap one bit."

"The ropes are for your own protection," Seer Jonah said. "Who knows what I might do to you if you attempted to interfere with our holy ritual?"

"Ritual?" Chloe said. "You wanna perform a ritual? What kind of a ritual?"

"Yeah, what's this all about, Drake?" Nick asked angrily. "I really need to frigging know and the impatience is almost killing me?"

Drake nodded. "Well, have any of you guys—and girls, of course," he added with a laugh, "ever heard of the other *Book of Atrocities?* I mean, the real one?"

"Huh?" Chloe's eyes narrowed. "Drake, what the hell are you talking about? There's another *Book of Atrocities?*"

And so Drake Melville explained.

CHAPTER 17

Drake + Ensemble Cast

Drake Melville nodded at his captives. "Yes, there are *two* Books of Atrocities. The one I have—meaning the one that I just got done writing—and the one that I don't have. But which I definitely intend to get."

He snapped his fingers. "Jade, my laptop please."

The winged woman nodded and then walked off through a doorway, her sneakers pattering softly across the stone floor, with the peak of her baseball cap looking like a beak. Everyone waited patiently for her return, which didn't take long. She handed a bulky laptop bag to Drake.

He showed the laptop bag around to everyone. "My version of the *Book of Atrocities* is in here. Thought out, typed in, edited down and backed up on numerous media in case of power failure. Now I just need the other one."

His point apparently made, he took three steps to his right and placed the laptop bag on a long trestle table that also bore cartons of Styrofoam lunchboxes and drinking straws.

"Just so we all keep it in mind that *this* isn't the book we're talking about," he explained with a gesture at the laptop. "Earlier, when I said I'd have the world at my feet, I wasn't referring to this *Book of Atrocities*." He looked at his captives. "Nod if you get this part."

Silence and nods all around; including from Melody and Liz.

Once certain everyone was with him so far, Drake smiled warmly at Jade. "Alright, hon, now you know the plan. You go tend the counter out there and ensure no one comes in to disturb me."

She nodded, but then raised a questioning eyebrow.

"Yes, I know the signs should discourage customers today," Drake added. "But you know how some folks can't take a hint. And besides, a member of staff who forgot his pack of condoms or her favorite dildo might still turn up to collect it."

Jade nodded again. Eyes flashing like green lanterns, she waved to the two bound women. "Goodbye, ladies, I doubt I'll be seeing either of you again. But not to worry, I'll be a great third wife to your husband."

Drake rolled his eyes. "Jeepers, you can always trust a woman to let the cat out of the bag."

"Or the dick out of the fag," Seer Jonah laughed, gazing at Melody's fear-shriveled penis.

"Huh?" Drake looked confused at the statement. "What dick and what fag?"

"Just impolite after-breakfast conversation," Seer Jonah replied with a wink. "Now, Drake, you were saying?"

Drake nodded and turned back to Jade. "So off you go now, dear."

Jade grinned at him. "Can I come back in after a while? I really would like to see this." While speaking, she puffed out the front of her gray halter top as if she was feeling hot.

Drake's eyes turned hard and cold. "No you can't. We stick to the plan. You know like I do that we can't let anything screw this up for us. So just keep watch out there. Don't come in here no matter what you hear, except you hear me calling for you personally."

The angelus nodded meekly and left.

"That's quite a cute chick," Seer Jonah said as she exited the doorway, her brown wings brushing its edges. "Too bad she doesn't require salvation."

"Sometimes she talks too much," Drake said. "But I guess all women do." He returned his attention to the captives. "So . . . where was I?"

Todd smirked at him." Before your McDonald's chicken bitch left us, you were about telling us why your jerk ass needs two copies of the *Book of Atrocities* instead of one."

Drake's lips twisted down at the insult. "One more comment like that, Todd, and I'll kill you and have Seer Jonah rape your corpse." He turned to look at Nick. "I'm sure my sister's ex can handle your camera just as well as you."

Todd glared at him but said nothing.

"Oh, for hell's sake get on with it, man," Nick growled. "Or do you plan on killing us with suspense, or what?"

"Yes please, Drake," Chloe added. "Please explain what this is all about. My wrists are beginning to ache."

Drake nodded. "Sure. Hey, what the hell—I'm more impatient than you are to get this over with." Then he seemed to calm down a bit. "Ok, so where was I?"

"Dude, you haven't even started yet," Nick pointed out. "All you've so far done is drop your laptop on that table."

Drake nodded again. "Alright, so back to the beginning then. Just so you understand what I'm going to do, I'm going to have to explain a few occult facts. First off, I need to tell you about the LOTUS."

"That's just a flower, isn't it?" Chloe asked.

Drake shook his head. "No. This LOTUS is an acronym for Library of the Unholy Sciences. It's sometimes also called the Necromantica—you know, the book of *necromancy*. But that too is an inaccuracy, promoted by people who either don't know the truth or who want to protect said truth."

"So, like Pontius Pilate once asked: What is the truth?" Nick asked with a scowl on his face.

"If you keep from interrupting me, I'll get there faster," Drake replied. "Just give me your undivided attention for five minutes and you'll understand everything."

"Well, as much of it as you'll be able to understand without making years of necromantic study like Mr. Melville has," Seer Jonah interjected. An evil smile on his lips, he looked back at Liz and Melody, who were both shivering now, even though the storeroom was very warm. "I'm sure the wives want to know even more than you do what Mr. Melville intends doing with them."

"Yeah, yeah whatever, tattooed dude," Chloe interjected in some irritation. Then she stared pointedly at Drake. "Okay, big brother, shoot goddammit, but hurry up. I need to go pee soon."

So Drake went on: "Now, no one knows for sure how big the LOTUS is— I'm of course referring to the necromantical library. But as everyone knows, libraries contain a vast number of volumes." He shrugged. "Some magicians say they are 666 books in the LOTUS, but that's mainly a conservative estimate touted by Satanists and antichrists for whom the number 666 has personal significance. A more realistic estimate would be 6,666, but other magicians, including the greatest of them all—by whom I mean both Ola Mimi and the magic queen Erin De Mornay—claim a much higher number of books in the LOTUS: 66,666 in fact."

"Damn, that sure is a lot of books!" Nick blurted out.

"I dare say it is," Drake agreed with a cool smile. He licked his lips and ran fingers through the pale hair over his left ear. "And there may even be more books than that in the LOTUS, because they are rumors that this demonic library stores magical records of, not just the evil of Earth's universe, but of all the parallel universes combined. In which case numbers may well spiral up to six-million-plus or even six-billion-plus or six-trillion-plus volumes, depending on how many universes there are altogether, and as several magicians have speculated, the number of parallel universes may well be infinite."

"So let me guess," Todd said after lighting up a new cigarette and taking a deep drag on it. "You want to perform a ritual to bring all those magical books to this room. Don't you think you'll be a little cramped for space in here? Or maybe that obvious fact just didn't occur to you and your two mentally-challenged friends?"

Drake rolled his eyes at Todd, who was languidly letting out two thick streams of smoke through his nostrils. "Please, please, stop doing your best to make me kill you," he said. "I've already told you, man: all I need you do right now is film everything that happens in here, and you can go home to your wife and children. Now, something that simple has to be really hard to fuck up, but you appear to be doing your best to rile me."

Drake looked at Seer Jonah and then laughed very loudly, his laughter seeming to fill the storeroom. "Okay now, tough guy, I'm going to up the ante. Here's the new rules we're playing by. If you dare piss me off again—just once, mind you—I swear by all the devils I believe in, that I will hand your family—your precious wife and children—over to Seer Jonah to use as sex toys."

Todd was so shocked by this threat that his cigarette fell from his lips. Then sputtering angrily, he rose from his chair with murder in his eyes, but was restrained by the cuff around his ankle. He strained with all his strength, trying to move the chair he was cuffed to, but it was firmly bolted to the floor and didn't give an inch. "How dare you threaten my family, you fucking son of a bitch!"

Drake's voice rose to match Todd's in volume. "Hey, you will damn well shut up and stop interrupting me . . . or else Seer Jonah will nail your children's heads together using your wife's arm and leg bones as the nails, and then he'll make condoms out of their intestines to fuck your sisters with. If you've read *The Bleeding Oysters* you might remember this was the punishment meted out to Alexis Craven when she rightfully accused Seer of raping her. Well, that wasn't fiction as the world believes. No, it actually happened. I was there and I saw Seer rape the bitch. And in addition, I was one of the judges who acquitted him of the crime—I never liked Alexis Craven, the dumb prude deserved what happened to her. And afterwards, we the jury kept Alexis's severed head—which was still alive, by the way—and made her give us blowjobs—cunnilingus for the ladies, of course—as additional punishment for wasting our time in court."

Drake stared coldly at Todd. "Now whether Seer does it again to *your* family is your choice."

"Bullshit!" Todd growled.

He still looked enraged and belligerent so Drake snapped his fingers at Seer Jonah. "The jar, man, the jar!"

Seer Jonah whispered a few words into the air. There was a bright flash of black light around his hands and then he was suddenly holding a large specimen jar. There was no liquid in the jar, just a woman's severed head. No doubt about it: the head was alive. The victim's eyes were wide and staring, her mouth moving, her lips opening and silently pleading for a mercy that would never come. All her teeth had been pulled out, but the wounds hadn't healed; her gums were a mess of bleeding tissue.

Drake laughed in amusement at his captives' shocked faces and gestured like an impresario. "Yes, ladies and gentlemen, this is all that remains of Alexis Craven, whom—I assure you all—is still very much alive in her jar and is now a very seasoned cocksucker also, one of the best of all time, in fact." He grinned at the jar, in which the terrified female head begged and begged in inaudible words, blood and spit running from her mouth, along with something that may or may not have been semen. "Now, Todd, I have many more magical jars like this one, indeed enough for your wife and daughters, for your mother and aunts, and your sisters and their girl children. So get it through your thick skull what I'm getting at here: which is, don't you dare goddamn fucking piss me off, asshole."

Nick gaped in horror. Chloe leaned as far forward as she could and vomited.

Todd sagged back into his seat, all the fight instantly gone from him.

After smiling at the defeated war veteran, Drake turned to Seer Jonah and nodded. Jonah whistled and the jar and severed head instantly vanished.

Nick heaved a sigh of relief. Chloe was dry heaving now, all her breakfast on the floor by her feet, with some of it splattered on her shoes. Drake waited for her to collect herself and sit upright again.

No one said a word until she did. After what they'd just seen, none of them dared speak. It wasn't just the brutality of the sight or Drake's story of how the woman's head had gotten into the jar that had them cowed, but rather the demonstration of supernatural forces that they had just witnessed. Todd and Nick were seasoned reporters, tough men used to covering violent crimes. But not 'magical' violent crimes. In the world they knew, a woman's severed head didn't plead with you to kill it, which was clearly what Nick had lip-read the bodiless Alexis Craven saying.

Chloe was gasping for breath now. She already had enough carryover sexual issues from her own rape. She hadn't needed to see this.

Todd seemed like he would burst with frustration. He was a man of action, and now he saw a need for action, a need to rectify a huge wrong, but he could do nothing about it. While the chain around his ankle and the threat of supernatural harm to his family both restrained him, he was as powerless as the others.

As powerless, in fact, as the two women gagged and tied up by the opposite wall, who were both now crying because they too had seen the living head in the jar.

In the meantime, Drake had turned back toward his bound wives. "I hope you darlings are paying attention," he said. "Because really, the two of you are the stars of my show."

His words provoked a fresh burst of tears from both women, both of whose cheeks were now striped like zebra crossings by their dripping mascara.

Shrugging, Drake turned away from them.

Chloe was back upright again. Drake gave she and Nick a no-nonsense look. "Now that that's settled and your macho cameraman's best behavior is assured for the foreseeable future, let me finish up my explanation." He frowned. "Yes, yes, like Todd pointed out, there's no space in here for the whole LOTUS library. But I don't need the whole goddamned library. I just need one book from the library: Volume 913, a.k.a. the *Book of Atrocities."*

After pausing for effect, and also apparently to make sure that no one had any further annoying questions, Drake continued: "You see, people, Volume 913 isn't like any of the others. The other books in the LOTUS deal with the usual black magic stuff—hurting and healing, summoning spirits to do one's bidding, destroying, killing, controlling others, and routine stuff like that. But Volume 913 contains the ultimate spell, the spell which will enable the speaker to control all the worlds." Drake frowned at the rather anticlimactic effect this revelation had on his listeners. "Yeah, yeah, I know you've heard this before—or at least watched it on TV—but this is the real deal, guys. Remember what I said out in the dining hall? That I'll have the world at my feet? Well, this is how. Once I get Volume 913 of the LOTUS—or Necromantica, if you prefer—I'll have godlike powers; *that* is the book's uniqueness." He smiled at them, thoughts of glory reflected in his eyes. "Yes, *godlike*. I'll be powerful enough to kick Lucifer off his throne if I so desire."

"But we're not interested in Hell," Seer Jonah said. "Just Earth."

"Hell's a nasty place," Drake agreed. "All they ever do there is torture people. Needless to say, once you've shoved a pitchfork through a few folks' guts or impaled an old woman or two, it becomes old hat, as routine as working for the post office. So, Satan can keep his realm. But our planet? It's ripe with possibilities for the man who can make it his own." He grinned at Seer Jonah. "And with the help of a few friends . . . ?"

"Drake, you can't be serious!" Chloe said. "This is crazy."

He nodded at his sister. "Yes, on the surface, it does look that way. But, success always validates one's efforts. Hitler is vilified today only because he lost World War Two. But what if the Nazis had won the war?"

"The ends justifies the means, you mean?" Nick asked.

Drake nodded. "Exactly. Of course, there are dangers to the process of acquiring Volume 913 of the LOTUS. I could accidentally erase both this static world and ours. Or, even worse, create a gateway for devils to flood into both and massacre everyone." Frowning, he shook his head. "That's why it's taken me so damn long to get things ready—I'm not here today to make any mistakes. I want to turn our planet into my version of Paradise, not end or ruin it for everyone."

"Man, you're sick!" Todd exclaimed. "You need a whole asylum of shrinks."

This time, however, Drake, caught up in his visions of glory, either didn't hear Todd or chose to ignore the insult.

"Don't do this, Drake!" Chloe pleaded.

Smiling tenderly, he leaned over her. "But I must do it, little sister. It's the natural thing to do: Earth must evolve, and I, Drake Melville, am its evolution. I will be the most powerful man in human history." His eyes glowing with either enlightenment or madness, he frowned and straightened up again. "But good things never come easy, of course. And locating the *Book of Atrocities* is no different. Confirmed by countless written accounts through the ages, everyone agrees that the *Book of Atrocities* is missing."

"And you've found it here?" Chloe asked, her eyes clearly revealing her hope that he hadn't.

Her brother shook his head. "No, it's still missing. But I intend to summon someone who'll definitely know where it is."

"Who's that?" Chloe asked. Nick and Todd had both fallen silent now, Nick deciding that Drake had merely succumbed to psychotic megalomania; while Todd recalled Drake's threats against the womenfolk in his family.

"Why, God Almighty of course," Drake replied.

That answer got everyone staring at Drake again.

"You-you-you intend t-t-to summon God Almighty t-t-to th-th-this place?" Nick sputtered. "Man, listen to yourself! Are you nuts?"

Seer Jonah laughed and shook his head. "No, he's not nuts. It can be done. Man is merely a nightmare in the mind of God. When that nightmare becomes too troubling, God will awaken to see what it wants, and will grant its request so He can slumber peacefully again." Jonah's facial tattoos seemed to have brightened now, both the black one above his upper lip and the pair that replaced his eyebrows, their 'I WILL SAVE YOU' message all the more alarming now that one had heard and seen the magic he was capable of.

"I don't expect you to take my word for it," Drake said and then gestured around the storeroom. "But hey, that's why you're here. You three are going to have front row seats for God's arrival in the human world. And Todd is gonna film it." He turned and walked over to his bound wives. "And unfortunately, Liz and Melody are going to participate in it." There was genuine tenderness in his voice as he said this, and while speaking he stroked both women's black hair, though each flinched at the contact as if a snake was biting her.

"What are you going to do to them?" Chloe asked him.

He turned back to face her, and now his face was sad. "Unfortunately, the ritual to bring God to this realm—confirmed, mind you, by years of research—requires my sacrificing two women that I love with all my heart. Two women that I've both loved and have had sex with." He glanced back at Liz and Melody. "Which means these two beautiful ladies." He sighed. "I was still in love with Liz when she left me, and in many ways I've never gotten over her. And of course, I love Melody to bits."

Chloe gaped at him. "And yet you're going to sacrifice both of them? Two women you still love?"

"The end *always* justifies the means. I must perform this ritual. So . . . yes."

"Oh, thank God I'm only your sister. This is just too atrocious."

Drake nodded. "Exactly. *Atrocious* is the word. And this atrocity, this betrayal of my own heart's truth will so offend God Almighty that he'll be forced to show up and hand me what I want."

Chloe sat back in her seat, stunned and silenced by her brother's callousness.

CHAPTER 18

Nick

It was crystal-clear to Nick Sinclair that Drake was mad.

Summon God, by sacrificing your two wives to him?

True, Nick only went to church on social occasions nowadays, but he was originally from the Bible Belt, and he'd listened to loads of preachers—behind the pulpit, on the radio while driving around, and on TV—and he didn't recall ever hearing any televangelists saying the way to God was by killing your loved ones.

He's nuts! He's a raving lunatic and we're tied up at his mercy! Damn!

Nick looked down at himself. Wrists tightly bound behind the bolted-down chair, feet duct-taped to the chair's front legs, and a pistol—Todd's loaded Glock—a mere yard away from his right foot. It was frustrating as hell.

Nick felt very foolish for not suspecting that the drinks Jade had served them out in the restaurant might have been drugged. *Dammit, I should have realized something was wrong when Drake didn't just meet with us at his house across town!*

He stole a glance at Todd. Todd was still silent.

I don't blame the guy. He's most likely still seeing that head in the bottle. Okay now, illusion or not, that was creepy. We really gotta stop this dickhead before he can do similar things to other women!

Drake was still raving and laughing in their faces: ". . . Words painted on Liz and Melody's backs are a single spell. Once both women are burned up in the fire—a living sacrifice as it were—the Gates of Heaven will open up and God Almighty will step through them and do my bidding."

On hearing that they were going to be burnt up, Liz and Melody Melville began howling behind their gags. In her shock Liz bit her tongue; blood trickled out from behind the duct tape and ran down her chin. But possibly because of Seer Jonah's threat to cut off their tongues, neither woman removed her gag to protest. Melody actually seemed about to tear her gag off, but then, catching a warning glance from Seer Jonah, she dropped her hands away from her face again.

" . . . Of course, there were other, even more strenuous preparations to do. Seer Jonah helped me immensely, in fact . . ."

Nick tuned the madman out. None of what Drake was saying mattered anymore. What did matter was saving Drake's ex-wife and current wife from being roasted alive. He looked over at both women again, and his heart flipped with pity for them. How in the world could anyone think that murdering two women he'd loved—no, the asshole claimed he *still* loved them—would bring God Almighty to him?

Nick's one hope at the moment was that there were no fires in evidence in here. Which probably meant that Drake intended to 'sacrifice' Liz and Melody in the McDonald's' kitchen, which was certain to have several large gas ranges.

Once they untie us to move us out of here, Todd and I can jump these two sons of bitches and subdue . . . oh, shit!

He'd just remembered that Todd's camera was set up to record things here in the storeroom, meaning . . . *We ain't going to the kitchen, are we? The murdering will be done in here. So where's the kindling and the wood then? Or is the guy just gonna douse those poor women in gasoline and fling a match on 'em? He seems crazy enough to do it!*

His mind fiercely at work now to avert two murders, Nick Sinclair began looking around the McDonald's storeroom. He saw no cans of gas, but then . . .

Hey, that black curtain just moved!

The black curtain on their right, and which covered that entire wall, had just twitched. While Nick watched, the curtain shook again.

There's something alive behind there? What the hell?

More worrisome, however, was the idea that there might be an incinerator furnace hidden behind the curtain, just like the arrangement in some funeral homes when the dead person was to be cremated.

But furnaces don't move by themselves. Which means someone is standing between the curtain and the wall, or maybe we're only using up half of this room and there's a whole unseen magical setup on the other side of that damn black curtain, complete with a coven of witches and maybe even more winged women in love with Drake Melville! And yes—I just smelt it again—that faint smell of raw meat! And it's coming from the area of the curtain, not from those walk-in freezers behind us. Hey, what's going on over there?

He ripped his mind away from the curtain's strange motion and tuned it back to their abductor. He'd been so lost in concentration that he'd not heard a thing Drake had said in the interim, but now the madman seemed to be rounding up by arguing with his sister.

"Don't do this!"

"But I have to, sis! It's for both of us! When I'm president of the world, you'll be First Lady. No . . . Jade won't ever stand for that, and that girl eats jealousy for breakfast—in her case the green-eyed-demon is merely the tip of the iceberg. I can't keep eyes in the back of my head to ensure she doesn't murder you. Okay, you can be vice president then."

"Drake, stop joking! What you're about to do is murder, pure and simple. It's madness. God doesn't want that from you, or from anyone!"

Drake laughed at that. Todd still wasn't saying anything. Todd seemed to be riveted on fixing something on his camera's tripod, which suddenly seemed a little shaky.

Nick though, tried to chime in his two-cents-worth: "Come on, man, be reasonable here. What kind of a god do you summon by roasting your two wives?"

The madman only laughed. "God Almighty, of course."

"By murdering your own family? By murdering two women you claim you still love?"

Drake Melville laughed. "Like God, I too work in mysterious ways. Seer Jonah hurts people to bring them closer to God. I will hurt people to bring God closer to me."

Even to Nick, who wasn't sure God actually existed, Drake's logic sounded crazy, a lunatic's justification of his insanity.

"Dude, you don't have to do this," he protested. "If you're so intent on meeting God, can't you just pray like everyone else does? Or become a priest or something?"

Drake smirked. "Faith takes too long. I need immediate results. Besides, God doesn't seem to hear the cries of the faithful anyway." Then he frowned and consulted his watch. "But enough of this idle chatter. We're wasting time here. I don't want Jade to start wondering why it's taking me so long to kill these two women and marry her." He glanced at Seer Jonah. "Time to pull back the curtain."

Seer Jonah crossed to the black curtain, took hold of one of its folds, and with a single forceful jerk, ripped the entire curtain away from the wall.

Nick gaped at what was revealed. He'd been quite wrong; there was no right extension to the storeroom over there. It was just a wall there; and what had been moving the curtain was the odd individual standing beside the corpse nailed upside-down on the wall.

On seeing the corpse Liz instantly shrieked in horror—the sound loudly piercing her gag. Nick glanced over at her and she had more tears in her eyes, was weeping a river.

He turned back to gape at the corpse nailed to the wall. It was an old man's corpse; the guy's hair was all white and gray. Nick felt like puking as his eyes took in all that had been done to the old man.

The view was completely insane. In addition to being suspended upside down, the old man's arms were extended sideways while his feet were crossed at the ankle and nailed together. Any doubts that this was intended as a mockery of Christ on the Cross were immediately cancelled out by the cross that had been created on the wall around the corpse: an upside-down one, of course, and one made from the dead man's intestines and other shredded innards, which had been stretched around him and nailed in place with what looked like spikes of bone to create the shape; ribs actually, hammered into the wall. Bleeding chunks of heart and lungs and liver and strips of skin were clearly apparent in the cross-shape, as were kidneys. (Nick had heard that humans had over fifteen feet of intestines in their bodies; now he believed it.) The old man's head looked like it had first been cut off his body and then replaced: its attachment point to his neck was a messy line of bloody tissue.

And then on to the most insane part of the entire sight. The entire interior of the dead man's torso had been hollowed out. There was nothing inside him—no flesh, no bones, and definitely no organs—between his shoulders and his pelvis. Nothing at all, just an oval hole through which one could see the gray storeroom wall.

The corpse was positioned such that the hole in it began about three feet above the floor.

Chloe let out a long moan of fright and fainted. Todd was still angrily fiddling with his tripod stand. Melody was staring bug-eyed at the insanity on the wall. Liz was fighting hard against her bonds, trying to get free. And now, rather than being too scared to ungag herself,

Liz seemed to be too infuriated to remember why she couldn't vocally express her anger.

Drake Melville and Seer Jonah were meanwhile staring at the excavated old man crucified inside a cross made of his own innards with satisfaction on their faces.

Nick managed to tear his eyes from the horrible sight on the wall and stare at the creature standing beside it. The thing was a giant—at least seven feet tall—but now that Nick looked more closely at it, he realized that it was actually a child. A giant 'young boy' of about five years old. And apparently the giant kid wasn't exactly compos-mentis. He was drooling spittle from one side of his mouth and his eyes glittered bright with idiocy. The kid was clearly mentally challenged. He wasn't chained to the wall or anything like that; just seemed to be standing and waiting for instructions. Craziest thing of all? The giant child was wearing Mickey Mouse pajamas!

Kid looks like there's aliens flying spaceships in his head!

"And now, everyone," Drake said calmly. "I'd like you to meet both my ex father-in-law and my son Frankie, both of whom have kindly agreed to help me summon God."

While they digested that information, Drake stepped back until his back was almost touching Liz, whose bound hands were reaching out to grab him (and most likely strangle him). Then, after seemingly making a few mental calculations, and while the weeping and distraught woman behind clutched frantically at him, he took a few steps forward again, knelt down and drew an invisible circle on the floor with his hands, and then once more stepped back.

Drake now spoke a few words to the ground, and next thing Nick knew, there was a large hole in the floor; a hole about three foot in diameter. And this wasn't any normal hole either. While they all watched, a circular stone wall grew up around the hole to a height of three feet.

Nick at first thought he was looking at a well. But then Drake whispered something else and fire blazed up from the hole—hot sulfurous flames that Nick could feel and smell from four yards away.

"And now that Hell's oven is open to receive my offering, it's time to begin," Drake announced.

"Oh fuck, no!" Nick gasped and began tugging against his bonds, desperate to get free before the madness really took off.

CHAPTER 19

Todd

Todd had stopped listening to Drake's ranting long before Nick had. Ever since Drake's announcement that he was going to summon God Almighty to this room in the back of a McDonald's restaurant, Todd had figured all their lives would soon be forfeit if he didn't do something. Drake had that crazed look in his eyes that men got when they'd tipped over the edge. Todd had seen that look before, more than once. He'd seen it during his time in the army; seen it in serial killers he'd interviewed in the state penitentiary; seen it in drug addicts; and even seen it in politicians, candidates for public office.

The upshot of this was that Todd Wilson knew he had to do something fast, or else . . .

He was having major issues with all this magic stuff Drake was pulling off though. He'd just managed to keep his sanity on realizing they'd been transposed to this place, but then meeting that winged Asian girl Jade? And then that living head in the jar? Even without Drake's threats against his family, Todd had major problems with seeing that head, with the semen and blood dribbling from its lips.

And now, the giant kid and the murdered old man on the wall, and the well of fire that had suddenly opened up in the floor. How was any of this even possible?

Duh, this guy is supposed to be a hack writer, not goddamned Merlin the Magician!

And maybe the others hadn't noticed it yet, but those weird tattoos of Seer Jonah's kept flickering on and off like Christmas lights, normally when he was amused at something. It was enough to drive poor Todd out of his damn mind.

Todd feared for his sanity if this continued. He wanted to return home sane to his wife and kids, not raving and needing to be locked away in a straitjacket. This goddamned madman Drake Melville was threatening to make a madman out of him too.

But not yet. Hell no, not yet.

Unknown to Drake and Seer Jonah, there wasn't a thing wrong with the tripod of Todd's camera. Not a damn thing. What had happened was, Todd had figured out that if he loosened one of the slim metal pegs that kept the tripod's legs in place, he'd be able to pick the handcuff around his left ankle with it. He'd gotten the peg free and had been fiddling with the cuff for about five minutes now. The problem was that he was having to rely on trial and error to get it open. So that he didn't alert their captors to what he was doing, he couldn't look at the damn cuff; he had to stare at either Drake and Jonah, or (what he'd finally switched to doing) pretend to be trying to adjust the stand.

It was a nerve-wracking process, and each time Seer Jonah looked at him, Todd felt a cold shiver run down his back. Because, if Drake was a megalomaniac, Seer Jonah's 'crazy' was of a different sort—Seer Jonah actually *believed* his own hype. Which Todd felt was much worse. To his mind, it was better to be a charlatan than a fanatic. A charlatan knew he was deceiving others; a fanatic was himself deceived.

Finally though, just after the fire-well appeared in the floor, Todd felt (more than heard) the click he'd been waiting for from the cuff. Relief swelling in his chest, he now seemingly gave Drake his full attention.

This had to be timed right. Todd needed to get across to his gun before the two madmen were able to stop him. He had to cross about twenty feet of space, which included dashing behind both Chloe's and Nick's chairs. The way he figured it, Drake wouldn't be able to reach him before he reached the Glock and chambered a slug, but Seer Jonah definitely would. And from watching Seer Jonah (for instance, the effortless way he'd ripped that entire black curtain off the wall with a single tug on it), Todd had realized that the slight-looking man was deceptively strong. He didn't want the pair of them getting into a punch-up; that would give Drake sufficient time to get involved too and maybe knock him out, or worse.

So when to make his move? Todd figured the best thing was to wait for a moment when both men were distracted. Which seemed about to happen as Drake turned from looking at his one-time father-in-law (damn, how could anyone do that to another person—carve a hole through their body like that?), and stared at his two wives instead.

"Alright, girls, it's time for you both to meet your maker."

Todd tensed. Drake stepped towards the bound women. Seer Jonah though was still looking at the captives, with his attention focused primarily on Drake's unconscious sister. He had a look on his face like he'd love to rape the woman. Todd figured that was for Chloe's brother to worry about.

"Seer, give me a hand with Melody, wilya?"

Drake was already loosening the rope that secured Liz's hands to the wall. Seer Jonah turned to assist him. Todd waited until the man was halfway across to Drake and then made his move.

He slipped the cuff off his ankle and dashed towards his gun. As good fortune would have it, Todd soon realized he had even more time than he'd expected. Clearly not in as much of a hurry to die as Drake was to kill her, Liz Melville was making a major nuisance of herself. Todd winced himself when she swung her bound arms like she was aiming for a home run and whacked Drake in the crotch. She clearly didn't emasculate him, because Drake remained on his feet, but the distraction was enough to let Todd pause behind Nick and undo the rope around his wrists.

"Don't let them know you're free," he whispered to Nick. "Just in case something goes wrong for me."

Nick nodded and Todd slipped past him and picked the Glock up off the floor. He was about to chamber a round, but then remembered he'd already done so back at Drake's house.

He pointed the gun across the chamber. "Hey, Drake, I've a message from God for you!"

"What?" Drake turned around and looked towards the camera, saw that Todd wasn't there and then let go of the fiercely struggling Liz to look for him.

Todd wasn't the sort of man to waste time or opportunities. He fired the moment Drake made eye contact with him. Todd wanted the man to know that he was going to die; and die by his hand.

But fate clearly had other ideas on the matter. It was crazy how this now played out: Todd had gotten a clear shot at Drake's head lined up, but just as he pulled the trigger, Liz hit Drake in the side of the head, knocking him off-balance and making him fling up his hands to right himself. Todd's shot thus hit Drake in the right forearm.

Drake howled in pain. Todd was trying to aim at his head again when he realized that Seer Jonah was charging at him.

Todd was a man of quick decisions. He saw the murder in Seer Jonah's eyes, swung the gun to cover him instead and pulled the trigger.

The bullet hit the tattooed sonofabitch in the belly, but didn't slow him down. Todd didn't get that; these damned slugs would stop a bull in its tracks.

Still, no time to reflect on that; Jonah was still coming at him; his eyes gleaming with pain. No, not with pain. With a shiver of fear, Todd realized that the wounded man was delighted; delighted that he'd now get his long-desired chance to hurt Todd in those obscene and creepy rites of his.

"I will save you, Todd," Seer Jonah said, and the black tattoos above his lips and eyes gleamed in obsidian agreement.

Todd had a very good idea of what Seer Jonah's idea of 'salvation' entailed. Hell no, he wasn't having that. "Save yourself, douchebag!" He fired again.

This time the shot did slow Seer Jonah down. The bullet hit him high in the chest, but it still didn't stop him. And the guy was bleeding funny anyway. His blood was all dark, not like real blood at all, but thick and gooey like molasses.

Startled, Todd tried to shoot again. But Seer Jonah had already reached him. The tattooed man grabbed Todd's gun arm and forced it upward, so that his next shot hit the ceiling and ricocheted off somewhere.

While wrestling with Seer Jonah for possession of the firearm, Todd heard Drake mutter a series of curses. A quick glance across the storeroom showed Drake trying to hold on to Liz, who'd just punched him again. Clearly no longer scared of having her tongue cut out of her mouth, she'd also now ripped her gag off and was screaming at Drake:

"Keep away from me, you goddamn crazy sonofabitch! How can you do this to your own damn family, you piece of shit!? Crazy bastard! Your own wives and your own son and father-in-law!? How!? How!?"

Todd returned his attention to his own battle. But his short lapse of concentration now cost him dearly. Suddenly he felt a horrible pain in his right arm.

Howling in agony, he looked down at his arm, his gun dropping from his fingers as he did so.

Shit, this tattooed sonofabitch has broken my arm!

Todd had no idea how Seer Jonah had managed it, but his right forearm was now bent at a right angle, with both bloody ends of both forearm bones jutting from their foursome of wounds. He looked up again and stared Seer Jonah in the eyes.

"It ain't over yet, asshole!" he growled at the man, flinging a left-handed punch at his head.

"I will save you!" Seer Jonah said with glee, and as he chopped Todd on the side of the neck, his red tattoos seemed to flare up in delight.

Todd's eyes rolled up in his head and he collapsed unconscious.

CHAPTER 20

Liz

Liz Melville fought with all she was worth. She fought like a she-wolf protecting her cubs. No way in hell was this sick bastard she'd once been married to going to sacrifice her to his devils!

Liz didn't know which was worse: her own current predicament or what he'd done to her father and son. Each time she glanced over at the room's far wall, where her father was nailed upside down with that crazy hole hollowed out of him, she felt as if her mind was imploding.

How could he do that to dad? And to Frankie?

This was just like in her dream, when she'd seen the black phantom creatures enter her son and transform him into a monster that had then killed her father. But hadn't that merely been a dream! Hadn't it?

Well, at least her son was alive. But this was another horror: 7-foot-tall Frankie, still as autistic as ever; still looking like he'd rather be watching cartoons on TV.

Liz had to get away from this madness before it consumed her.

Drake had already freed her hands. He hadn't loosened them, but to move her to the hole in which the fire burnt, he'd had to fully untie the rope connecting her wrists to the wall. He'd just gotten through doing so when Todd had made his escape bid. That distraction had enabled Liz to startle Drake. And once Todd had shot him, she'd also managed to bend down and untie her ankles. But then, just as she'd turned to run, Drake had grabbed her arm.

"You're not going anywhere, honey. I need you for this!"

"In a pig's eye, asshole!" She'd kicked at his balls, but he'd been anticipating this and had gotten out of the way. So next, Liz did the obvious thing: she brought both hands down hard on Drake's gunshot forearm. That had worked good: he'd immediately screamed and let go of her.

Time to go, Liz thought.

She glanced at Melody. Melody was staring pleadingly at her; her eyes begging for help. Liz wanted to wait and untie Melody but there simply wasn't any time for her to do so.

Sure, Drake was hurt at the moment, but he wasn't down and out. Even if Liz got Melody's hands free from the wall, there was no way she'd be able to unbind her ankles too before Drake grabbed her again.

And then there was also Seer Jonah to consider. She'd so far been lucky that Seer Jonah was occupied with Todd, but once the two of them finished their fight . . .

"I'll fetch help," she whispered to Melody. "Don't worry, you'll be safe till I get back. Remember he said he can't use just you; he needs me too for his ritual."

She turned away from Melody and took off running. She had to get to the door and out of this hellish McDonald's restaurant.

Once free from this place, she had no idea what she'd do; but whatever it was, the results couldn't be as bad as being sacrificed.

She ran for the door that Jade had exited from. That one was certain to lead to the outside. And at first it looked like her luck was good; no one came after her.

But then she heard Drake yell: "Frankie, go bring your mommy back! Hurry!"

And that was what tripped up her escape attempt. Liz was already at the door and working the lock—thankfully Jade hadn't locked it from the outside—when she heard Frankie's thudding footsteps arriving behind her.

"Mommy, come back!"

His voice was the same as always and it broke Liz's heart. Hadn't she come here mainly for a cure for his mental issues, which she was now certain Drake was responsible for?

No, she couldn't just run off and leave him. She'd take him with her. Yes, that's what she'd do. So Liz turned around and looked up at giant Frankie with love as he pulled up in front of her. Despite his present huge size he was still her little son; still wearing the blue Mickey Mouse pajamas that she'd bought him, although the chest area of the pajama top was sticky with drool. Disgusting lines of black tar dribbled from his nostrils and ears, as if the nightmare creatures were still hiding inside his body.

But he was her son! She couldn't leave him behind!

So instead of yanking the door open and fleeing from him, she ran to him and grabbed his hand. "Come on, Frankie! You and mommy will escape together!"

But the giant kid—and oh, he completely dwarfed her now— pouted. "Not want to escape! Want to play death with you and daddy!"

Then he leaned forward and picked her up. Lifted her as easily as she usually lifted him.

She fought against him. "Let me go, you little brat! Put me down at once! Go play with your father if you want to, but put me down right now. Right now or else there's no ice cream for you!"

But maybe Liz Melville shouldn't have used the ice cream threat on Frankie. Because it was clearly what led to what happened next.

Dammit, Drake, you God-damned fool! she thought in horror as her upset son wrenched her head off. *You should've told him not to kill me! The boy watches cartoons all day long. And mentally deficient as he is, he probably thinks humans are like dolls that can easily be put back together again!*

Liz was of course dead before her son began pulling off her arms and legs too. Then, looking very serious, he shredded her torso as well.

And only then, when his mother was completely dismantled and couldn't try escaping anymore, or try taking his ice cream away from him either, did giant young Frankie Melville gather up her remains and take them back to his father.

CHAPTER 21

Nick

Nick gaped in horror when the giant kid walked back into the chamber clutching pieces of his mother's body to his chest.

He'd heard Liz screaming, but had thought she was merely protesting being recaptured.

But this gruesome sight?

Oh my God, Nick thought.

He was relieved that Chloe was out cold. No way did she want to see this.

The kid was covered in blood now, his pajamas were a complete mess.

Creepiest thing of all? The giant boy seemed to have no idea of the gravity of what he'd done. He just walked up to his father and held out his arms, which caused several pieces of Liz to drop to the floor, her head included.

"Caught mommy for you, daddy," Frankie said. "Brought mommy back to you."

Now it was Melody's turn to faint. Frankie was standing close enough to her that when Liz's intestines slipped out of her belly, they plopped down on her bare feet. Melody shrieked and slumped to the floor, the rope tied to the wall keeping her arms suspended above her head.

Drake meanwhile, was staring at his son like he was about to have a fit. Nick found it almost comical how angry Drake looked.

Even Seer Jonah looked shocked by this unexpected turn of events.

"Oh my God, what have you gone and done, son," Drake asked the giant boy, craning back his head to look up at Frankie.

"You said catch mommy, so I catched her for you," the child replied in all innocence. Then he grinned and blew giant spit bubbles from his mouth. "Now I go put mommy back together so we can play the death game!"

That said, he bent down and tried to gather up the spilled chunks of his mother's corpse. But this didn't work out, as each time he picked up one piece of her, he wound up dropping two or three others.

"Look, son, pick her up in sections," Drake instructed, wincing when Frankie dropped most of Liz's torso and it rolled over and he saw the ruined runic inscriptions on it. "Take your mommy over by that wall and assemble her there like your Lego set. No no, not all at once or she'll just spill everywhere again. Take what you've got in your hands first and come back for the rest. Put her down near Grandpa, but not too close to him."

"Okay, daddy," Frankie agreed. "But do I get ice cream after death game? Mommy said no ice-cream. I WANT ICE CREAM!"

"Yes sure, sure, whatever flavor you like," Drake said, slapping himself on the forehead in exasperation. "I'll ask Aunt Jade to get some for you. And if there's none in the fridges here, she'll fly back to the house to fetch it for you."

"Okay, daddy," Frankie repeated and began moving his mother's pieces towards the wall.

Staring after him as he went, Drake looked mad enough to kill the giant kid. As did Seer Jonah.

Well, that seems to have put a damper on his plans for world domination, Nick thought.

Liz's death hurt Nick a lot. He'd known her to be a very nice woman. She'd been a kind person, a woman dedicated both to furthering her acting career and to raising her son well. She hadn't deserved to die like this, messily shredded like a loaf of bread. No one deserved to die like that. And it was this asshole Drake's fault.

Nick glanced down at Todd.

Todd was regaining consciousness but was still stunned; his eyes were as crossed as Frankie's. A pool of blood lay around his shattered arm, the sight of which made Nick wince.

He's out of it for now, Nick thought grimly. *It's up to me to save us now.*

He was relieved that he'd kept to Todd's instruction not to let Drake and Jonah realize that his hands were free. Nick's hands were still clasped behind his chair.

He glanced at Chloe to see if she was rousing from her faint; but she wasn't. She was still out cold; rendered unconscious by the shock of seeing the old man nailed to the wall.

Next, Nick stared at Todd's gun, which had fallen not far from its original position, about a yard and a half from his chair. Then he looked up at Seer Jonah, who was gazing down at Todd with an evil light in his eyes. Seer Jonah didn't seem to notice that he had two bleeding bullet wounds in his torso; with the one in his chest being quite close to his heart. A thick line of blood also dripped from a wound between his shoulder blades.

Their eyes met and Seer Jonah laughed.

"Some people just can't take a hint," the tattooed man said. "Your friend wasn't marked for salvation today, but now indeed I must save him from himself. I must deliver him from his own stupidity. It's a wonder that any woman could love such a man as this. So I will be saving his wife too—saving her from the grief of growing old with him."

These words were spoken with deep conviction. Seer Jonah sounded so logical that Nick almost nodded in agreement with him. But he managed to refrain himself from doing so.

Something is really wrong with this guy, he thought. *That's not blood he's bleeding—looks more like maple syrup. And why, oh why are his damn tattoos now glowing like frigging LEDs? But more important, how do I work this now? I already know not to make the same mistake Todd did in underestimating this guy. But if I'm going to move I'd better move fast, while Drake is still pissed off at the giant kid. Yes, we've saved the world from his megalomaniac designs, as it were; but he might still kill me and Todd in retaliation.* He looked away from Seer Jonah and down at Todd. *Hell no! Me, I ain't taking any chances: when I shoot this Seer freak it's gonna be in the head!*

There was still a problem though: Nick's feet were still duct-taped to his chair, and that meant the gun was still too far off to reach. So, just like Todd had earlier, Nick now needed a distraction of some kind to tip the scales of combat in his favor. Either that or Todd would have to lend him a hand and nudge the gun his way. Which wasn't about happening, because it was Todd's right hand that lay near the firearm; and with the way that forearm was damaged (Nick winced again when he looked at the ninety-degree break in the limb and its exposed bones) he wasn't about using that hand for a while.

But Nick also needed to do it quick. Because Seer Jonah had now turned from staring at Todd's prone body to staring at his friend instead.

"I would like to save this man from his sins," Seer Jonah told Drake. "Is this acceptable to you, or do we still need him?"

Startled by the unexpected question, Drake looked up from his shot forearm. Viewed through the veil of hot air that wavered around the flaming well in the middle of the room, he looked weirdly distorted.

"Dammit, Seer!" he growled, "you could have waited till I was done with this."

"You were busy? I apologize."

"Yes, I was trying to repair my shot arm. I was almost finished with the healing spell. Now I'll have to start over." He looked over at the wounded war veteran on the ground. "Yes, you can save him if you so desire."

"I do desire it."

"Yes, yes, save him then. He's proven to be more trouble than he's worth." He glanced meaningfully at Nick. "Nick will operate the video camera for us when we conclude the ritual."

This was news to Nick. *Conclude the ritual? Oh, we haven't saved the world yet? But how not?* But Nick had noticed that Seer Jonah also seemed to have gotten over his anger at Frankie's unscripted killing of Liz.

A healing spell, huh? If Drake can fix his own wounded arm, maybe he can also reassemble Liz and still use her corpse? Or has he just remembered that his magic books say the corpse doesn't need to be in one piece, and he can just dump all the parts of her into the fire?

"Please, Seer, don't interrupt me again," Drake said. "This gunshot wound frigging hurts like hell and I'm losing a lot of blood."

"Okay. But I would suggest that you also shield yourself from further harm," Seer Jonah said. "Overconfidence can kill you. Remember that, Drake. Always remember that."

Drake nodded. "Yeah, thanks, I *will* shield myself now. I should've done so at the start of this."

Drake turned away to concentrate again on whatever it was that he was doing to his arm. Nick flexed his fingers behind his chair and starting planning on how to get to Todd's gun before Seer Jonah could 'save' Todd.

Oh no, you sicko, you're not gonna . . . !

Seer Jonah had meanwhile hooked his fingers under Todd's armpits and was pulling him towards the fire. Todd went along so meekly—like he was a rag doll—that Nick began suspecting that the vicious chop to the neck he'd suffered had partly paralyzed him. This seemed to be confirmed when he made no resistance when Seer Jonah dumped him right next to the well of fire and then bent down and began undoing his belt.

"No, no, no!" Todd quietly groaned, his feet kicking out weakly as Seer Jonah slid his pants and underpants down to his ankles. "No, no, no!"

Seer Jonah laughed away Todd's protests. "Yes, stubborn sinner. Now I will save you. Oh yes, I will!"

"Hey, let go of the man!" Nick shouted as Seer Jonah now rolled Todd over and parted his buttocks and began examining Todd's anus with his fingers.

Seer Jonah looked up at Nick and laughed loudly. "Why are you scared, little man? It is not *your* day for deliverance yet."

Nick wanted to scream at Seer Jonah, but found he couldn't, because right then Seer Jonah's clothes all melted off his body. They didn't catch fire and burn up; no, they dripped off of him like melting plastic, forming a multicolored puddle on the floor.

That in itself was scary enough. But there were two additional things about this scary scenario that *really* scared Nick.

First of all, all of Seer Jonah's tattoos were now glowing. Both the red ones that spiraled his body from toes to shaven skull, and the black ones over his lips and eyes. All of them pulsed like neon lights, making Seer Jonah seem semi-divine.

The second thing was that Seer Jonah had a massive erection. His penis was also covered with glowing tattoos, which made the organ look like a dangerous weapon; something capable of shredding flesh like a knife. The man's penis seemed as hard as a rock, and Nick realized what he intended to do to poor Todd.

Todd, of course, was still flat on his belly, and couldn't see Seer Jonah spitting on his penis and smearing the spit over the organ's fat head. Todd was fighting to move his arms and legs, but his limbs weren't cooperating much with him. His fingers clutched weakly at the side of the flaming well, but he seemed unable to grip anything or turn himself over. The room was hot enough as it were, but from being right next to the source of the heat, Todd was now sweating profusely. His intense perspiration had glued his shirt to his muscular back and his bared legs dripped water to the floor.

Seer Jonah kept spitting on his erection and lubing it up.

"Stop it!" Nick yelled at Seer Jonah. "Don't do that to him!"

"I will save him!" Seer Jonah said gleefully when his penis was dripping spittle. "Salvation comes from agony. I will hurt him so much that God will have no choice but to pardon him his sins, which I am certain are very many, for he is a very headstrong man. And stubbornness is as the sin of witchcraft!"

Nick had thought that anal rape was 'all' Seer Jonah had in mind for Todd, but of course, he was very mistaken. A man—no, a monster—of Seer Jonah's depraved capacities would never consider a 'mere' rape worthy of 'salvation.'

What Seer Jonah did instead, was to lift Todd up and place his head and shoulders—his entire upper body, in fact—into the fire coming from the well. And then, while Todd caught fire and his body was roasting, that was when Seer Jonah began raping the screaming man.

Todd, his hair on fire, was screaming blue murder. His shirt was burning and his body had already begun giving off an odor of roasting meat. Meanwhile, Seer Jonah labored away at Todd's backside, and blood quickly began dripping down his own legs from Todd's torn anus and rectum.

Nick couldn't see Drake now; Seer Jonah was in the way. It didn't matter though: Seer Jonah was so caught up in 'saving' and sodomizing the screaming Todd that he never noticed Nick hurriedly untaping his feet from the chair. While freeing himself, Nick thought he'd go mad from the sound of Todd's screams. He glanced at Chloe, wondering how she could remain unconscious through all this racket. But she was still out cold, slumped in her chair with her head drooping to the left; her body prevented from sliding to the floor by its bonds.

Then Nick's legs were free and he leapt for the gun. He scooped it up and rushed over to Todd and Seer Jonah.

It was clearly too late for Todd. He wasn't dead yet, but would soon be. Viewed through the flames, his agonized face was a roasted and sizzling sack of meat and his eyes had long since exploded. The charred skin on his torso had cracked open and the blood that dripped from those cracks instantly sizzled in the hellish fire and boiled away as steam.

Seer Jonah was singing to himself while he sodomized Todd. He had a firm grip on Todd's hips and he lustily swung himself in and out. There was a wide pool of blood on the floor between his legs. The tattooed spiral on his scalp almost seemed to be on fire now; that's how brightly it was glowing.

"Look out, Seer!" Drake called out at the moment Nick placed the gun to the back of Seer Jonah's bald head. "Look out, he's got a gun!"

Too late. Nick pulled the trigger four times in quick succession.

Seer Jonah's head exploded into pieces.

Nick blinked in surprise. For a moment it seemed to him as if Seer Jonah's head and body weren't true flesh and blood, but were composed of a liquid, swirling blackness.

And then the dead man fell forward into the burning well and was gone, along with his victim.

As the joined men vanished into the fire, Nick had the disgusting follow-up impression that the red words tattooed on Seer Jonah's penis had been glowing on the outside of Todd's ass.

Nick couldn't peer into the well, but a loud noise—the sound of an explosion in Hell perhaps?—shortly reached him, along with a simultaneous jetting of blue and black flames from the mouth of the well, flames which smeared black across the storeroom ceiling, and which seemed in danger of setting the place on fire if they spread over to the stacked cartons. But after an initial mushroom-cloud flare-up, the raging flames died down again, the roasting heat in the room returned to normal, and after grimacing at the pool of blood by the well that marked Todd's rape, Nick found himself staring across the room at an irate Drake Melville.

He smirked at Drake. "You know, your tattooed friend should have taken his own advice and not gotten overconfident."

Drake seemed too angry for words. He kept staring at the flaming well as if he expected Seer Jonah to emerge unscathed from it—which Nick was certain wasn't going to happen; not after seeing that violent plume of black flames that had burst forth from the stone ring.

Hell no, dude. Your friend's gone for good, down to where he rightly belongs. Good riddance to the ultimate in bad rubbish!

There was something very strange about Drake now, but Nick didn't know what it was. He could see though, that Drake's previously gunshot arm now looked completely healthy again.

Uh uh—that ain't good for me!

He did the logical thing: took aim careful at Drake before he got his wits back and pulled the trigger thrice.

The bullets bounced off of Drake. They ricocheted away as if he was made of stainless steel. One slug even zipped past Nick, less than a foot away from his head. Another thudded into the inverted corpse on the wall, causing giant Frankie to look up curiously from his task of trying to reassemble his dead mother.

Nick stared at Drake in amazement. *What's going on now!?*

Not sure how many shots were left in the gun, he lowered the weapon and studied Drake to see what was different about him.

Then it hit him: *A shield! Seer Jonah told him to shield himself.*

Nick could clearly see the demonic 'shield.' It ran in a thick black line around Drake, making him look like a cartoon drawing.

Nick stared at Drake in confusion. Drake turned from staring at the well to stare back at him. Drake had apparently not even realized that Nick had been shooting at him; he was that traumatized by the loss of his friend Seer Jonah.

Now he realized why Nick looked so confused. "Forget the gun, man. So long as I'm shielded like this, nothing can hurt me."

Nick looked down at the gun, looked back up at the thick black outline around Drake, and winced. *He's right. Dammit, he's right!*

It was at this point that Chloe woke up again. "Oh, dammit!" she growled. "What's with all the noise and gunfire?"

CHAPTER 22

Chloe

Once Chloe was fully awake, the changes in her environment quickly registered in her mind. At first glance, the most apparent of these was the burning well that now occupied the storeroom's center.

How the hell did that thing get in here? she wondered as she stared in horror at the orange flames that wavered and danced within the stone ring. She wondered if maybe she was still asleep and dreaming. But no, everything else in here was the same, except for . . .

Hey, where are Todd and Jonah?

Chloe saw no sign of either man. Then she realized that Nick had somehow gotten free and was holding Todd's gun. Looking past Nick, she saw that Melody alone now lay bound on the ground behind her brother.

Which of course made Chloe question where the three others were.

And then a loud childish voice jerked her attention right, to the wall where Drake had crucified his father-in-law upside down.

The childish voice was singing: "And all the king's horses and all the king's men couldn't put mommy together again. Yes, all the king's horses and all the king's men couldn't put mommy together again."

Seeing her giant young nephew sitting there trying to reassemble his mother, a look of serious concentration on his face as he scrambled the ten or so pieces of her around on the ground in front of him, almost made Chloe faint again.

Tears filled her eyes and she yelled at Drake, "Have you gone raving mad!? What is wrong with you!? What are you doing!?"

She was so loud that Nick turned to look at her. His face was strained, as if he'd been through hell while she'd been unconscious. He was also sweating profusely, positioned as he was beside the strange flaming well in the middle of the storeroom.

"You okay?" Nick asked her.

She nodded back, grateful for his concern. "Hey, where's Todd and Seer Jonah?"

He pointed. "Gone for good, down the wishing well."

Chloe now noticed the two puddles of blood on the floor; one near Nick's former chair, the other one right beside the burning well. She looked up into the dancing flames, and winced on grasping what Nick meant. *Oh, poor Todd.* But she also felt intense delight that that creep Seer Jonah was gone and wouldn't be back. She'd hated the way he'd kept leering at her.

Then, remembering that Nick had the gun and currently held the upper hand over her brother, she said, "Hey, please untie me. My arms have gone numb."

Nick took a step towards her but then halted when Drake called out, "Hey, not so fast! We still need to conclude the ritual."

"Ignore him and untie me," Chloe said in irritation. "*You're* the one holding a gun here."

"Your brother is bulletproof now," Nick said, which statement made no sense to Chloe. *Bulletproof? How can anyone be bulletproof?*

She stared across the room at Drake, who still had on just his tee shirt and jeans. "Hey, Nick, I don't see my bro wearing any Kevlar."

She began to feel really mad. "Just get me out of this damn chair, will you? And then I'm gonna put that jerk brother of mine in this place."

Of course, while speaking Chloe had no idea how she was going to put Drake 'in his place.' She just knew that someone had to, and realized that her guaranteed immunity as his beloved sister meant she could slap the crap out of him without any fear of consequences.

Nick took another step towards her.

"I said stop!" Drake ordered again in a voice dripping with menace.

Nick did stop, but then he turned around to Drake and gave him the finger. "Screw you, man. Don't you get it yet? Liz is dead; you've lost. Give it up already."

Drake laughed and walked around the well of fire towards them. Chloe now noticed the thick black outline all around his body. *Is that . . . ? What is that? Bulletproofing?*

Drake stopped a few feet from she and Nick, at whom he scowled dismissively. "Lost? No, I haven't lost, you fool. I'm just getting started."

Nick rolled his eyes. "Man, you said yourself that the ritual requires you to sacrifice two women whom you both love and have slept with." He pointed over at the wall, where the seated Frankie was still singing moronically and wondering why he couldn't 'put mommy back together again.' "Drake, Liz is *dead* . . . you know, like in D . . . E . . . A . . . fucking D . . . ?"

Then Chloe noticed that a horrible thought seemed to hit Nick, because his eyes widened and he first looked down at her, then back up at Drake. "Aw, c'mon, man, you're not going to use your own sister, are you?"

Drake laughed at them both. "Why the hell else do you think I asked her to come along? As backup, of course." He too pointed over at his giant son. "In case something like that happened."

Chloe gaped at him in horror. "Drake, you're my older brother. You can't sacrifice me. You can't have sex with me! That's incest."

Drake nodded and a cold smile curved his lips. "Darling, the end always justifies the means. Besides, after sacrificing you, once I'm all-powerful I can always resurrect you as a zombie. Not as good as true life maybe, but being undead is better than nothing."

"You . . you bastard!" Then Chloe fell speechless and just struggled against her bonds, while Nick stared glumly at his gun as if wondering what was wrong with it.

So I guess Drake really is bulletproof after all? she thought.

"Hell no, Drake!" she spat when he took a step in her direction. "I'm not letting you rape me. If you dare bring your dick near me, I'll—" She couldn't say for sure what she'd do to him if he tried to rape her, but she was certain it would be excruciating and might render him incapable of ever having sex again.

"But I don't need to rape you, darling sister," Drake said with a smug smile. "I've already slept with you."

Hearing that, Chloe stopped her raging and gaped at him.

Nick also gaped at him. "You've what?"

"When?" Chloe asked breathlessly. "Tell me, when?"

Drake shrugged. "Oh, back at that party where you were gangbanged. When I came in and saw you all naked like that, I couldn't help myself. You looked so beautiful like that, and I'd always madly desired you, so I quickly unzipped my fly and helped myself too, before I called Tessa Lau and we both revived you. And I wasn't disappointed either. Despite the crappy circumstances, you were a fantastic lay."

Chloe was speechless. Amidst the general craziness of this situation, she now felt her world start to fall apart. The knowledge that Drake—this brother whom she idolized—had betrayed her so fully stabbed her in her heart. It was devastating to realize that their entire relationship was a lie. Even if she could forgive him for sleeping with her when she was drugged-up (and in light of his support afterwards it *was* possible—deep in her mind—to rationalize his actions as resulting from his intense—if misplaced—love for her), it was impossible to forgive the fact that he'd intentionally lured her here to sacrifice her. This second betrayal negated everything between them. They were less than family now.

Suddenly Chloe was furious. "Drake, you slimy bastard, I'm gonna kill you!"

He pointed at her bound feet and then crossed his wrists over each other and shrugged, so that she clearly understood he was referring to *her* bound wrists, not his free ones. "I don't see how you can."

She got a good view of his supposed 'bulletproof shield' now. Though in profile it seemed like a black line, when you looked directly at Drake he seemed to be wrapped in a plastic membrane, like twenty or more transparent bags placed over each other. It really was odd to see, as if he was standing in a skin-tight shell of water.

Frustrated, Chloe turned to Nick. "Shoot him. Shoot the damn waste of skin."

Nick looked helplessly back at her. "I already did. Didn't work."

She wasn't satisfied with that. "Are you just gonna let him get away with this?"

In response to her question Nick threw a punch at Drake. Despite its imperviousness to bullets, the shell must have had some weaknesses, because Chloe saw it dent and let Nick's hand through.

The punch rocked Drake, who flinched and staggered back and almost fell over. But then he straightened up again, scowled angrily at Nick and whispered a spell at him.

Nick instantly froze in place. Chloe watched the anger on his face as he tried to get free to hit Drake again. But he couldn't even raise the gun in his other hand.

Drake nodded at Nick. "That's ended your little rebellion. Now I command you to walk over to Todd's video camera and record everything that is about to happen here. I want God's arrival caught on camera."

His face twitching with useless rage, Nick nonetheless instantly began walking towards the video camera. As he stepped past Chloe's chair, she got the feeling that someone else was in control of Nick's limbs. He was walking like a robot, like a puppet on strings. Even the Sesame Street muppets moved more lifelike.

She watched him step behind the camera and sit down, then place his eye to its viewfinder. Once in that position, his body froze there, like it was a factory automation awaiting new software commands.

She turned back to stare at Drake, who was looking down at her with compassion on his face. His gaze made her uneasy; he seemed really sorry.

"Please, darling sis," he said sadly, "I really didn't expect it to come to this. And just as with Liz and Melody, I want you to realize that my ability to use you in this ritual is final proof of my sincere love for you. Chloe, dear, I truly do love you from the bottom of my heart."

She glared up at him. "Love, and you're doing this to me? Oh, how I hate you now, you bastard!" she shouted. "You'll surely burn in Hell for this!"

"But you first," Drake replied sadly with the ghost of tears in his eyes. "And when you get there, tell old Lucifer that I'll be along too—maybe—in a few million years."

Chloe was about spitting in his face when he touched her forehead and her mind went almost completely blank.

All she was able to do after that (while he magically pulled her out of her chair without even loosening her bonds) was belatedly wonder how in the hell her elder brother had become so versed in the supernatural.

CHAPTER 23

Nick

There are moments in one's life when one feels completely helpless; when it appears that the elements—the very atoms that comprise the universe—are working against one.

For Nick Sinclair this was such a moment. His current state of being felt worse than being paralyzed. He had the creepy sensation of being trapped inside a container named 'himself,' his body now an object that belonged to someone else, and which was also controlled by that person. And this was no idle comparison. While he'd been walking over to the camera, he'd actually felt something that wriggled like worms inside his limbs moving them.

Throughout his career as a journalist Nick had always smirked at supposed cases of demon possession. The Devil had merely been the bogeyman that preachers used to make the faithful open their wallets. But now . . .

As if it was psychically bonded with his mind—the 'thing' that was now running his body gave him freedom to adjust the video camera, but that was all. Any attempt to desert his current post left his limbs as dead as those of a monkey hit by a tranquilizer dart. He'd brought the gun along with him, but the evil controlling force had made him drop it by his feet before it had glued his face to the camera's viewfinder. The tripod had at first seemed wobbly, but then the same force that had stiffened Nick seemingly stiffened it too.

So he watched and recorded, first of all sweeping the room to catch images of the crucified granddad with the hole in his body, and the retarded grandson who sat a few yards from the corpse, and who was still singing his "All the king's horses and men couldn't put mommy together again" nursery rhyme.

It was now that Nick noticed for the first time that Frankie had strings of what looked like black licorice dangling from his ears and nostrils. He zoomed in to see better and saw that the black strings were wet and that they were wriggling, as if they were alive and fighting with one another.

Demon worms in the giant kid's head? Ugh, that is beyond gross.

At first there was little else to see. Chloe seemed to be unconscious when Drake lifted her out of her chair and carried her across the storeroom. After laying her down on the floor and ripping her clothes off, Drake pulled his wife Melody up from where she was slumped and arranged her beside Chloe, on Chloe's right. Melody woke up while being moved, and at first tried kicking Drake away from her, until he touched her on the forehead, when she suddenly become all zombie-like, like Chloe.

Then Drake walked off left, to return with a book and a black Sharpie.

The next ten minutes or so were taken up with Drake completing his spell again. This took a long time because the first half of each line had originally been written on Liz's back, with some words split in two across both she and Melody's backs, and so now Drake had to be careful to ensure he duplicated that exactly. Zooming in with the video camera, Nick could see Drake working with painstaking care to get the syllables at the split in the right places again. Nick wondered, but couldn't see, if the words were already split across two bodies in the book that Drake was copying them from.

He grew bored with this, and to pass the time, began thinking about the winged woman, Jade, who even now was tending the counter outside in the McDonald's restaurant, watching to make sure that no one got in here to disturb her future husband.

That's if he's gonna marry her at all, Nick mused. *Guy like this who'll use his own sister for voodoo? A snake'd make a more trustworthy spouse.*

But so far, despite all the gunshot noise in here, Jade hadn't made a coming-to-the-rescue showing. Nick knew she'd have heard the shooting; but it seemed that Jade was sticking to Drake's instructions to her to not to enter this room unless he personally called her in. Which meant she knew he could bulletproof himself if necessary.

Which is great for me, as one-on-one in a brawl is way better odds that two-on-one. If I can somehow just break free from this damn 'thing' that's holding me captive!

Drake finally seemed to get the spell inscribed to his satisfaction. Nick watched him straighten up and then stare around the storeroom, as if ensuring everything was set up exactly the way he needed it to be. He spent a long time looking at his murdered ex father-in-law, finally walking over there and measuring the hole cut through the corpse, estimating both its height and width with his hands.

Nick suddenly understood why Drake had tunneled through the old man:

Oh no! He's made a gateway out of the old guy! Once Drake sacrifices the girls, he expects the wall to open up exactly where that hole is and grant him access into another dimension; possibly even into Hell.

Then, staring at the flaming well in the middle of the room and realizing that *it* most likely descended directly to Hell, Nick corrected himself: *No no no! That's not what he plans. The madman really does expect Almighty God to emerge through the corpse.*

Nick trembled at the thought. It was so insane, too insane to be true. But in the past four hours—*Damn, have we really been here for just that short while*—Nick Sinclair had seen so many impossible things happen that he no longer knew what was possible anymore.

In his confusion, he found himself believing that maybe, just maybe, Drake Melville really would succeed in bringing God here.

Meanwhile, after a glance at his son, Drake returned to the two bound women on the floor. He knelt in front of them, peeled the duct tape off of Melody's mouth, and then touched both she and Chloe on their foreheads and whispered a word. Both women's lassitude immediately vanished and they began squirming and struggling fiercely on the floor where they lay.

However, neither of them could help herself, which once more made Nick wonder at Drake's magic prowess, because he now realized that when Drake had pulled Chloe off of the chair she'd been bound to, he had somehow managed to simultaneously tie her feet together in the process. And also, when he'd ripped Chloe's clothes off, each garment had come off her body whole, not shredded like one would expect. Her shirt, pants, bra and panties all lay behind her, each of them in a single undamaged piece; even their buttons were all still intact.

Were it not for the gravity of the situation, Drake would surely have been an amusing sight. Wizards and warlocks were supposed to wear gem-studded robes or defiled surplices to perform their evil rites, not faded jeans, Nikes, and Slain Jane tee shirts.

Staring at that tee shirt launched another question in Nick's mind: *Wasn't Drake supposed to have been in love with Slain Jane's lead singer Janet Orgasm? So much so in fact that he even helped out with several lyrics on the S.U.A.F.M. album? So how come he didn't invite Jane O along instead of Chloe?*

"Please, darling, don't do this to us!" Melody pleaded with tears running down her face.

"Yeah, let us go, you scumbag!" Chloe growled in anger. "You can't do this to both of us!"

"Please, honey, let us go!" Melody pleaded again. "I won't tell anyone about this. Promise! You know I really love you!"

Drake shook his head. "I'm sorry, darling, but no can do. You see, I'll never have another chance like this. It's statistically impossible that there'll be another time in my life when I have two women I truly love." He looked sideways at Liz's scattered remains and smiled sadly. "Three, actually. Wow, how lucky can one man be?"

Yeah, asshole, Nick thought in disgust. *All that love and you're just gonna throw it away like trash. Some folks don't even have one person who truly loves them; maybe not in their entire lifetime.*

"Come on, Drake, you can't do this!" Chloe howled at him.

"And now the screaming starts," Drake said, and with an excited look entering his eyes, he straightened up once more.

"Hey, come back here where we can see you!" Chloe screamed at him as he walked off behind them.

She and Melody both tried to turn around to face him, but before they could do so, Drake plunged his hands down between their naked buttocks.

Chloe and Melody instantly screamed.

Nick zoomed the camera in, first on their faces (to catch their agonized expressions), and then on their backsides. The way both women had screamed chilled him to his bones. . . . And just before Drake had bent over them, Nick thought he'd seen the man's hands turn black as coal, as if the demonic outline around him had flowed down to his hands and concentrated its essence there.

But that was nothing compared to the awful sight that awaited him once he got the video camera focused on Chloe and Melody's behinds.

Oh my God, no! He's dug his hands right inside their asses!

Chloe and Melody were still screaming and now Nick could see why: Drake's arms were buried well beyond the wrist in each woman's behind, and he was twisting and turning them in there, while blood gushed out of each woman like water from a fire hydrant.

When Drake stood up again, Nick felt like vomiting. Drake had hauled about four foot of intestine out of each woman's shredded anus. He stood there with the lengths of intestine in his hands and a maniacal smile on his face.

Needless to say, both Chloe and Melody continued screaming blue murder. Their shrieks of agony were so loud that Nick felt he was going deaf. The two women were making frog-eyes now, their eyes so bulged out that they might already be seeing Drake's God.

Drake let go of the intestines and dug his hands into Chloe and Melody's backs instead. And then, gripping their spines as if they were handles, he lifted both screaming women off the floor like human suitcases, and carried them towards the well of fire, while blood welled along their hideously exposed lumbar vertebrae and dripped down their sides, and those twin lengths of bleeding intestine trailed from their anuses along the storeroom floor.

Once more Nick felt like vomiting. He was sure the only reason he didn't expel the entire contents of his stomach was because the force that had frozen him in place, and which was now controlling his limbs, refused to permit it, rightly assuming that letting Nick throw up would interfere with his camera work.

Yes, Nick had witnessed expressions of terror, pain and despair on folks' faces in his life, but he'd never seen anything like the expressions of complete misery and agony on Drake's wife's and sister's faces as he raised them high over the edge of the flaming well and dropped them into its fire.

"NOOOOOOOOOOOO!" one of them screamed as she fell into the inferno, but was it Chloe or Melody? Nick would never know for sure.

At that moment, seeing those two women suffer such a terrifying and agonizing fate, Nick would gladly have sold his soul to the Devil for the chance to tip Drake Melville into those flames also.

Nick just stared. He couldn't believe he was witnessing this, seeing two innocent women being burnt to death. Two women whose only crime had been falling in love with the wrong man, a homicidal maniac with delusions of . . . Nick wasn't even sure what to accuse Drake

Melville of anymore. Megalomania? Yes, that sort of fit the bill, but one could also add religious mania, superstition . . .

But this isn't superstition, is it? None of this is make-believe in the least.

A horrible thought now came to Nick's mind: *Fuck! If this psychopath actually lays his hands on the fabled Book of Atrocities and winds up ruling Earth, we're all gonna be screwed but good.*

Once the gory human offering was made, the flames spurted up again.

This time, however, rather than the black fire that had accompanied Seer Jonah's demise, these flames were a mixture of floral purple, shocking pink, brilliant red and the purest white imaginable, as if the flesh, skin, blood, and bones of the two victims had not fallen down to Hell but had instead been converted into fire. The colors were so pristine, so pure, that Nick almost expected to see Chloe and Melody's tormented faces amidst them.

But that didn't happen. What did happen was that the multicolored fire looped up out of the well and rained down on Drake, who made no attempt to escape from it, but instead stood there and stretched up his arms as if in worship.

The next thing that happened was that the fire melted Drake's clothes off his body, while he stood there grinning amidst the shower of sparks, not harmed by them in the least. When the flames subsided again, looping up from Drake and then falling back down into the well, Drake's body burnt with flowing red lines of script. Nick had no idea if the words had earlier been tattooed on him just like those on Seer Jonah, or if the rain of fire had just created them.

"And now it is time!" Drake yelled at the ceiling. Then he turned towards Nick. "Make sure you capture all of this on film or I'll kill you and feed you to the well, just like I did to my wife and sister."

Nick couldn't nod because of the force now controlling his limbs, but inwardly he shuddered. Once more, he glanced longingly at the gun on the floor.

Dear God, if I could just reach that thing! Because now, either by accident or design, Drake's magical shield was gone. Actually, it seemed to have been replaced by the reddish glow that the script on his body was giving off.

But glowing like that didn't save Seer Jonah from death, and I'm certain it won't save Drake either.

The ritual continued. Now Drake Melville turned towards his crucified father-in-law, hung there inside that evil upside-down cross of intestines and shredded internal organs, and began chanting words in a language Nick had never heard before, but which he suspected was the one tattooed on Drake's body.

He acting like he's Moses receiving the Ten Commandments, Nick thought angrily.

He swung the video camera between Drake and the wall, but finally just kept it focused on the wall because something was beginning to happen there.

The wall was visibly altering. Not the whole thing—the area where Frankie sat playing with the body parts was still perfectly normal—but the entire area around his crucified grandfather seemed to be melting, with the corpse first fading into the stone and mingling with it, meat and stone mixing up like milk being stirred into coffee, and then the resulting amalgam dissolving backwards into the wall like plastic touched by fire.

A hole formed in the wall exactly where the hole in the old man's body had been, and then it spread outward, revealing a space beyond in which floated something blue.

He frigging did it! Drake really did it! Nick thought, though he wasn't as shocked as he'd thought he'd be.

And then the divinity beyond the McDonald's storeroom—God Almighty, according to Drake's gospel—began coming through the hole in the wall.

It billowed like gas expanding and twisted and coiled like a serpent.

The blue aura had been an effect of some kind, one possibly created by the creature's presence in the space it was emerging from. As it emerged through the wall Nick saw that its true color was grayish-brown.

What the hell? he thought on seeing that the emerging creature was a mass of tentacles and wings, with eyes and mouths studded at the base of its tentacles. In accordance with this description, it was completely shapeless.

Oops, now this is just wrong on so many levels, Nick thought in instinctive disgust. If not religious, he was at least familiar with the biblical statement that 'God created man in His own image.' *And that damn thing doesn't look the least bit like me.*

Worst of all, this emerging creature's body was rotting all over; both its tentacles and wings and the bare patches of skin between them bore huge pus-dripping sores. An intense reek of rotting meat came from it, and beyond that was a reek of something else; this second and more pervasive smell being something that made Nick want to flee screaming.

This creature that Drake had summoned—this 'God' as it were, reeked of complete EVIL. There was no other word for it: this creature was EVIL incarnate.

Now, Nick was a card-carrying agnostic, a guy who held Jesus and Santa Claus and the Easter Bunny on almost equal footing, but even he knew for sure that this thing Drake had summoned wasn't the Christian *Jehovah*, or the Muslim *Allah*, or *Buddha* or any of the Hindu pantheon of deities, or any other such supposedly holy being.

Hell no, this thing that Drake Melville has just called out of its home realm ain't in any way divine. This thing is an atrocity, an abomination; which kinda makes sense to me, seeing as Drake wanted the Book of Atrocities, right? This creature is frigging EVIL, EVIL made flesh—that fact is beyond contestation.

He smirked. *Well at least, this is a god that truly fits its worshipper.*

But giant Frankie seemed to think it was cute . . .

And Drake was indeed awed by it. He knelt on the floor like a Muslim at prayer and bowed to it.

"Oh, Master, great God of all the heavens and all the hells, thank you for harkening to my call. What I desire of Thee is the *Book of Atrocities* by which I will establish Your kingdom of darkness on Earth—both on this static world and on the spinning Earth that I come from."

Drake repeated this prayer of supplication and request three times, while the monster fully emerged from the wall. It was about the size of a pickup truck and hung there in midair like a chandelier, with its rotten tentacles waving and its putrescent wings fluttering. And it smelt like a roadkill convention.

Drake now got back up to his feet.

He stared at the thing he had summoned with delight on his face. "The book, Lord. The book! Give me the *Book of Atrocities* and I will rule this world and the other in Your name!"

Dammit, Nick thought. *Is this guy such a fool that he doesn't realize something has gone wrong? Or is he just so evil himself that this monstrosity's own evilness seems like holiness to him?*

The giant child Frankie had been watching all of this in delight, leaping up and down beside the wall and drumming on it with one of his mother's severed legs and one of her arms. Maybe it was the smell of raw flesh that attracted the creature, or maybe Frankie's agitated motion irritated it, but suddenly it flung out two tentacles as thick as housing pillars at the child.

"Hey, daddy, God is playing with me! He's tickling me!" Frankie shrieked in delight as the monster's tentacles wrapped around him. But then he began screaming in terror when the thing pulled him close to itself and, stretching its mouths out of its body, began biting huge chunks out of him.

It was only now apparently that Drake began to realize that something had gone wrong with his sacrifice and incantation to summon Almighty God.

The creature was still eating Frankie, pulling him to bloody pieces with even more ease than that with which Frankie had grumpily killed his mother.

"I'M FREE AT LAST! YES, I AM FREE!"

The words went off like a bomb in Nick's head. He knew it was the creature shrieking in delight. The words had no physical sound and had a grating texture unlike any voice Nick had never heard before or ever desired to hear again; it felt like someone was scouring the inside of his head with steel wool. He wished he could grab his head and cover his ears, anything to keep the atrocious voice out. Across the room he saw Drake cover his own ears, finally even falling to his knees again before the terrifying monster, who made another mental comment:

"THANK YOU FOR FREEING ME, DRAKE MELVILLE. I HAVE WAITED LONG FOR SOMEONE WHO COULD UNDERSTAND THE ANCIENT SCRIPT TO PERFORM THIS RITUAL AND SET ME FREE."

Drake managed to get back to his feet. He looked horrified. "Then you're saying this was all a trick? You're *not* God Almighty and you don't have the *Book of Atrocities?*"

"No, I do not have the *Book of Atrocities*," the ghastly creature replied him, this time thankfully in an audible voice; because Nick was certain that if it had continued speaking inside his head, his brain would have become pulp and squirted from his ears and nostrils.

"The *Book of Atrocities* is still in the library," the shapeless floating monstrosity that reeked like sewage went on. "I indeed searched for it, but there were too many books. Oh, too many books." It sounded scared as it made the latter statement.

"Then you lied?" Drake asked. "You're not God? Everything was a lie?"

"I did what I had to do to free myself, Drake Melville," the creature said in clear amusement. "I am EVIL personified. What do you expect? Truth from one whose truths are all untrue? I did what I needed to, and you . . . you did what your own evil nature compelled you to."

Its hundreds of tongues licked Frankie's blood from its countless tentacles. Several of its tentacles rolled Frankie's severed head about on the floor as if it needed something to distract it from getting bored while talking to Drake. Other tentacles extended sideways and began picking up Liz's remains and ferrying them to the creature's mouths. Its many wings fluttered as it hung there in midair, but Nick got the distinct impression that its wings were merely decorative; even combined, they were clearly no match for the creature's bulk; something else must be keeping it airborne.

"You . . . bastard!" Drake sputtered in rage. "You've made me kill the only three women I've ever loved!"

"Every quest involves risk and sacrifice, Drake Melville," the creature countered. "You may still find the *Book of Atrocities*. It is in the library somewhere. I think—"

But Drake was already charging at the creature, large black flames suddenly erupting from his hands.

"You cannot kill a god," the creature laughed in great amusement. "But I am grateful to you, so I'll not kill you either."

And that was when Nick felt the force that had paralyzed him lift. Suddenly he could move again of his own volition, and the first thing he did was bend down and grab the gun off the floor. Afterwards he realized that he'd acted on pure instinct. Had he expected to shoot the monster? Or had he simply thought he'd need a weapon to get past Jade, who'd be guarding the outside exit, while fleeing the storeroom?

He neither knew then, nor later understood his true motive.

The next thing he knew, a dark force had pulled him off his feet and was shuttling his body through the air at speed.

He tried to bring the gun up and shoot, because it was clear that he was heading towards the monster and was about to become another quick meal for it, maybe its lunch.

But then the demonic creature moved aside and Nick found himself flying through the hole in the wall through which it had emerged into the McDonald's storeroom.

Aw heck, no! he thought as he was dumped into an untidy heap beside Drake Melville.

He instantly leapt up again and ran towards the portal to escape this confinement, but the portal was now covered by a transparent plastic window—like flexible, stretchy glass—and in addition, had begun to shrink.

Nick acted on his first instinct. He pointed the gun at the window and fired, intending to shatter it. But other than the deafening noise that followed, nothing happened. It seemed to him that the bullet was absorbed into the window: on its impact there was a shimmering on the window's surface, and a few ripples like when a pebble strikes a pond, and then the see-through substance returned to normal . . . and continued shrinking.

Nick stared helplessly at the gun, then at the window.

Then, realizing he was now trapped in here, he stared instead at the horrible creature floating outside.

CHAPTER 24

Nick

"All that hard work and it didn't even bring the *Book of Atrocities* to me," Drake said in a small voice and walked over to stand beside Nick.

Nick ignored his voice. The main worry in his mind was that he was now trapped in here, while outside . . .

Outside in the McDonald's, the freed monster slowly began shrinking in size and altering in shape, until finally it looked exactly like Drake.

"That goddamn identity thief!" Drake growled in intense anger and frustration.

Nick too was stunned by the transformation. *How the hell is that possible?* he asked himself, unsure of how many times so far today he'd desired the answer to that same question. Because the creature out there was now an exact copy of the Drake Melville in here, down to the glowing red tattoos on his skin.

Nick could feel Drake's anger as an almost palpable presence beside him. He continued to ignore the man, however. What was happening outside their new prison was too riveting to ignore.

Outside, the transformed monster had now walked over to the table on which Drake's laptop bag lay. 'He' opened up the bag, looked the laptop over, and then zipped the bag up again. "Great, it truly is finished," he said.

His voice came through the flexible plastic barrier as if over a phone line, washed clean of its uppermost and lowermost frequencies, and at times crackly with static. Despite this denaturing though, one thing was clear—the monster was speaking in Drake's voice. And, listening to the creature—how 'he' sounded so far away while seeming to be close by—Nick had the strong feeling that he and Drake Melville were now both somewhere very far from home.

"This book will be my literary masterpiece," the monster said with evident delight. "Once it's published, the world will really bow at my feet!"

"Yeah, great!" Drake said with a scowl. "Now you're gonna steal my work and take credit for it, right?"

The see-through membrane, which had now ceased shrinking and remained about window-sized and at head height, appeared to only conduct sound inward however. The monster apparently couldn't hear them. Nick had no idea if 'he' could see them either.

"Is there any frigging way out of here?" he asked Drake.

Now it was Drake's turn to ignore him. The monster-Drake had just picked up Drake's cellphone and was studying it. A moment later, he put the phone to his ear and they heard him say: "Jade, honey, I'm done in here. You can come in now. And please bring me some fresh clothes."

Jade entered two minutes later. The short interval gave Nick the impression that she'd been waiting impatiently by the storeroom door and could have been summoned by simply yelling her name. But that would have meant she'd anticipated Drake's need for fresh clothing and already had some with her.

"Where is everyone?" the winged woman asked breathlessly, placing a pair of jeans and a white tee shirt on the table with the laptop.

"Dead, gone, whatever, wherever," 'Drake' said dismissively.

Try hard as she might, and she was obviously trying very hard, Jade couldn't help but look delighted by this information.

Nick chuckled at the expression on the winged woman's face. *Well, of course she's happy—this means all her romantic competition's gone. He's all hers now.*

"And the other *Book of Atrocities?*" Jade asked breathlessly. "Did you get it?"

"Sort of," the fake Drake replied. "I'll explain later."

Jade seemed confused by his answer. "Honey, are you certain there's no problem? I don't see any book here."

"Later, honey pie." Before she could question him further, he pulled her to him and kissed her, a move she responded passionately to, seeming to flow into his arms and melt against him, while her wings unfurled and stroked the air sensually.

"Oh dammit!" the real Drake spat beside Nick. "Now that sonofabitch demon is stealing my woman too!"

"Your fault, man," Nick replied unsympathetically. "If you'd not started all this nonsense, none of this would ever have happened." He frowned at the kissing couple and shook his head. "And from the look of things out there at the moment, I doubt she was ever really as concerned about your stupid *Book of Atrocities* as you were. I think the woman just wanted to be loved, and was scared you'd dump her for good if she didn't go along with your crazy plans."

Drake ignored him and paced off, his glowing body illuminating the stone floor of their prison as he walked back and forth. Finally, however, unable to restrain his curiosity, he stalked back to the plastic window and stared out of it again.

Jade and the other Drake separated from kissing.

"Hey, both of your wives are dead now!" she told him playfully, punching him on the chest and throwing a grateful look at the still flaming well. "Do you still love me? Are you still gonna keep your promise to me and marry me and take me to your own Earth to live with you?"

"Yes! Yes! Yes!" the fake Drake nodded. And then, while the real Drake groaned in frustration, the duplicate quickly spun Jade around and bent her belly-down over the table. He next tore off her black McDonald's work pants, pulled the pink thong beneath them aside, and slipped his erect penis into her from behind.

"Oh shit! That feels so damn good!" Jade gasped on being penetrated, while beside Nick, the real Drake Melville spat in anger, banged his fists against the impervious partition and began pacing again.

Nick wondered why his companion didn't just magic his way out of their confinement and go confront the impostor, but it was clearly because the monster's magic was greater than Drake's.

There was nothing else to do, so Nick watched the fake take Drake's woman, who clearly couldn't tell the difference between them. As the impostor thrust into her, her brown wings began flapping furiously, until he had to push her down flat against the table or else she'd have bucked him off of her.

"Yes, yes, yes!" Jade howled as their bodies stiffened together in orgasm.

"No, no, no, this is a total disaster!" Drake groaned as the impostor collapsed on his girlfriend. "Jade, you bird-brained bimbo—that's not me!"

"C'mon, dude, the dick has to feel the same to her," Nick said. "Or maybe she's just forgotten how yours feels in all the years since you last slept with her. How long ago was that anyway?"

Drake looked out at his girlfriend kissing the impostor and scowled. His answer was spoken more to himself than to Nick: "She knew it had to be that way. We agreed it had to be like this. If I'd kept sleeping with her, I could never have loved Melody like I needed to."

"But your own *sister* too? Man, how low do you have to be to do that? Why couldn't you just have asked Jane O to come along? Now there's someone who'll hardly be missed by anyone." The outspoken, bitchy, and 'publicly depraved' rock singer (Janet Orgasm had once claimed she didn't have a 'private life'—everything she did from waking till sleeping was intended for public consumption) was loved and hated in equal parts by the media; much like Drake himself. "So, why not just ask Jane along?"

"Oh, I didn't love her," Drake said miserably, watching through the window as his double put on the clothes that Jade had brought for him. "I tried to—but she was impossible to love. She was an incredible fuck, but that was all."

Nick honestly still couldn't get his mind around the idea that one could kill someone he truly loved merely to further his own selfish ends. It was insane. *Yes, that's right. It's insane. And Drake is himself insane to have even contemplated such an idea.*

Even weirder was the idea that this copy of Drake Melville—this demonic creature that was so evil that one could literally smell the wickedness coming off of it, would return 'home' to the 'Spinning Earth' and would successfully impersonate Drake Melville there. And who knew what would happen now when 'he' published the *Book of Atrocities*?

If Jade couldn't tell the difference between that fake Drake and the real one standing in here beside Nick, then who could?

And then things got odder still:

"Well, honey, I think it's time for your own makeover now," the fake Drake said. "Are you ready?"

"As ready as I'll ever be, darling," Jade said, her green eyes glowing with love for him. She was sitting on the table, with her wings draped over its edges, and now leapt down from there to the floor and grinned expectantly at 'Drake.'

And then he touched her on the forehead.

A spark of electricity leapt from his fingers and circled her head. Jade yelped and staggered back against the table, her wings beating furiously, as if she wanted to take flight and escape from 'Drake.' Nick at first thought that the creature had deceived her and was harming her, but this was soon shown to not be the case.

What happened next was that Jade's wings shrunk and vanished and her face and body changed too, until finally she'd become a perfect copy of Melody Melville.

"Hey, Drake, it really looks like you can't catch a break today," Nick said in amusement, as the replacement Melody Melville began dancing around the fake Drake in delight. She looked perfect, gorgeous. Even her little transsexual penis looked exactly the same as Nick remembered it. "Dude, I sure hope your monster double likes anal, 'cos he's just magicked the bird's pussy away."

"Shut up, man, or I'll goddamn turn *you* into a bird!" Drake spat back at Nick.

"Well, I guess the show was too good to last," Nick said as the window they'd been watching through now vanished. It seemed that the demonic creature had left the plastic aperture open just to taunt Drake Melville. The evil creature had wanted to impress on him the completeness of its victory: how it had taken over his entire life without there being a single thing he could do about it.

Nick also understood now that Seer Jonah had been lying when he'd said Drake didn't know the spell to open the portal out of the Static Earth.

Or maybe he was telling the truth, and the Drake in here with me really can't get back out unaided; but that new version out there almost certainly does know the way out.

Nick's shoulders slumped in disappointment. *So, out there, the replacement Melody and Drake Melville will be heading back to Earth. While in here . . . I'm stuck with . . . dammit!*

Nick was finally forced to pay attention to his own surroundings.

With the window into the McDonald's gone, the only light he had to see by came from Drake's glowing tattoos.

That illumination was more than sufficient however to reveal that they were both confined inside an oval room that was about twenty feet long and ten wide. It had no windows or doors, a weirdly carved floor, and stone walls that rose up to a domed stone ceiling.

Nick was suddenly flooded with panic. *We're trapped in here! Forever and ever.* But of course, even that was an exaggeration. *This room is completely devoid of furniture or food or water. And without water, we're both certain to be dead in less than a week.*

He stared angrily at Drake. "Hey, man, see what you've caused now with all your selfishness?"

Nick was very conscious of the gun he was holding and how easy it would be to vent his anger on Drake—to just kill him now. But three things stopped him from doing so. Firstly, because even though he'd watched Drake Melville murder two women and cause the deaths of at least five other people (he was now certain Bonnie hadn't left for Boston last night like Seer Jonah had claimed), he'd never killed anyone before and didn't think he could—he placed too much value on human life, even one as worthless as Drake Melville's. And secondly, Nick wasn't sure there were any bullets left in the gun he was holding. This second consideration was important because Nick was haunted by the memory of how easily Drake had dug his hands into Liz and Melody's backsides and ripped their intestines out of their bodies.

That was totally supernatural. If I try to kill Drake and fail at my first attempt, he can easily do the same to me; or even just rip all my limbs off and leave me to bleed to death here.

Nick's third reason was a very basic one. Simply put: he needed Drake. With the man's magical abilities, he might conceivably be able to get them out of this hole he'd gotten them into.

And this was why, even though Nick had been aware for a while that Drake was no longer wearing that demon-shield outline around him and was now vulnerable to harm, he made no attempt to kill him.

But doing nothing hurt him too. Thinking of Chloe's horrible death filled Nick's with bitterness. Like all the others who'd died, she'd been a nice person, completely undeserving of such a horrible fate. At one time he'd even loved her; almost as much as this idiot brother of hers claimed to have before so callously killing her.

His fingers tightened around the grip of the gun and he wished he had the coldness of heart to murder Drake, just like Drake had murdered all those people. Although in this case it wouldn't truly be murder, just a well-deserved execution.

Or do I just lack balls? he wondered. Then he directed his disgust outward again, at the man who'd caused so much pain and misery.

"So, Drake, what's your plan to get us out of here?" he asked angrily.

Their current situation was truly an odd one. Drake was all the light they had in here. He looked like a flickering statue or a neon sign. (Drake's penis was glowing with red letters too, but at least the guy didn't have an erection—Nick wouldn't have been able to cope with that.) Nick's cellphone was out in the McDonald's storeroom, along with all the other personal effect collected from them when they'd been taken captive.

Which in retrospect was weird, right? Why take away our stuff if we can't make calls here anyway?

"Hey, man, I'm talking to you. Say something!"

But Drake didn't reply. Nick was about prodding him into making a response when he saw why Drake hadn't replied him. Drake was looking away from Nick, staring down at the carved symbols which Nick had earlier noticed on the floor of their stone prison.

"Yes," he said to himself, as his glowing body illuminated the floor. "I knew it."

"You knew what?" Nick asked.

"That creature—the demon I accidentally summoned in God's place," Drake said, again sounding as if he was talking to himself rather than replying Nick, "he said he'd not kill me because I'd freed him. But there's no food and water in here, and soon we'll run out of air in here too—which would clearly spell death for me. . . . So, there has to be a way out of here. And this is it!" He crouched down and ran his fingers over the carved floor. "A pentagram! A magical circle. Hahaha! There is a way out. A sacrifice! That's the key! A human sacrifice! That's the reason he sent two of us in here, not just me. And now I'll—"

Nick saw he had no choice in the matter now. Acting without an ounce of hesitation, he lifted the Glock and aimed it at the back of Drake's head. Then, looking up, he whispered a silent prayer; he prayed for the first time in twenty years: "Dear God Almighty, if you truly exist, please let there be one bullet remaining in this gun. Or else I'm gonna be so fucking dead; and now that I know for certain that there's a Hell down below, I've no interest whatsoever in dying until I've gotten my business straight with you."

Nick pulled the trigger.

There was a loud 'Boom!' and Drake Melville's brains exploded out of the front of his head.

Nick felt nothing but intense relief as he watched Drake's body keel forward onto the magical circle carved into the floor.

I'll rather die in here of starvation and thirst, you bastard, than let you sacrifice me like you did the others!

Wanting to make absolutely certain that Drake was dead, he pulled the trigger again, but the hammer clicked on an empty chamber. The gun was empty.

"Thanks, Old Guy in the Sky, I definitely owe you one," he whispered up at the cave ceiling as Drake's body ceased its LED-like glow and the cave faded into total blackness.

But the cave wasn't dark for long.

The floor began glowing. Not the entire floor, just the place where Drake had fallen.

Nick stepped closer for a look. *What in the world is happening now? Hey, this guy ain't gonna pretend he's Jesus too now. The asshole ain't about resurrecting, is he?*

But it wasn't that. What was happening was, the pentagram cut into the floor was glowing as Drake's blood flowed along its lines, the blood emitting an even brighter light than his body had.

And then a voice spoke. It wasn't speaking English and wasn't audible to Nick's ears. But he heard it in his mind and understood perfectly what it said.

"Welcome to the LOTUS—the Library of the Unholy Sciences," the voice announced. "The magician's sacrifice is accepted and passage granted to the library's contents. I—the Voice of LOTUS— will now open the door for you."

In contrast to the demon-monster's overpowering voice, this one was soft, calming, and androgynous in both range and timbre.

Nick was stunned. He looked down at the glowing pentagram, now full of blood from Drake's shattered head, and shivered.

"Remove the body of your sacrifice from the pentagram and stand on it alone," the disembodied voice instructed Nick.

Nick did so, trying not to look at Drake's face—half of which was now missing—as he rolled him aside. Then he stood on the pentagram and said, "I'm ready."

He felt nothing and saw nothing happen, but the next moment he was standing on a similar pentagram in a large hall. This pentagram however wasn't bloody.

Nick immediately saw that he was indeed in a library. Oh, and what a library it was! Bookcases extended in every direction as far as the eye could see, and each one was piled with books from floor to ceiling.

What was it Drake said again? The LOTUS might actually contain millions or billions of books?

"Welcome once more to the LOTUS, sorcerer," the pleasant voice in Nick's head said. "Now that you are here, please feel free to avail yourself of all our facilities. Here you will find books on everything EVIL. The LOTUS, occasionally also referred to as the Necromantica, is the universe's exhaustive and most comprehensive collection of books on magic and evil lore . . . You are free to peruse and consult all the works of evil literature here. Be warned however, there is no Volume 913. The so-called *Book of Atrocities* is no longer kept here . . . Many have come seeking it, but all have left disappointed. Many years ago, the angels of God came and took the book away. No explanation was given when they took it."

Nick nodded in awe. There was something about these endless rows of books—these aisles stacked with routes to powers he wanted nothing to do with—that felt like a knife peeling back the layers of his mind like he was an onion.

The Voice of LOTUS was still speaking: "All contracts between humans and demons must be signed in human blood. I repeat—all contracts between humans and demons must be signed in human blood."

Nick nodded again while studying the library ceiling. Glowing yellow lights ran between each aisle of bookcases, making them look like runways to eternity.

"The LOTUS is spatially dislocated," the voice said. "You will neither age nor hunger or thirst here. For your relaxation there are bedrooms and bathrooms with both films and music. Once again, magician, I bid you welcome to the LOTUS. If you arrived here accidentally, you may be here a very long time."

Nick stepped off the pentagram. The library floor was of cold gray stone and seemed to welcome him.

"Do you require any specific help, magician?" the Voice of LOTUS asked. As far as Nick could tell, the voice was a software program; a magical AI program.

"I just wanna go home, man. Where's the exit door?"

"The only way out is the same way you arrived here. Of course this will require another blood sacrifice."

Nick had another question: "So . . . that monster who was in here earlier? How did it get out then?"

"How it returned to the waiting room? It killed another magician. It is permitted to do so." The voice paused for a few seconds, then added, "However, it may be possible to find a book among the many in the library with a spell to displace you to where you wish to go without the need to shed blood. This is very rare, but it is possible."

Nick gaped at the endless arrays of bookcases. "Where's the damn index?"

"There are many of them, located in different parts of the library," the voice said. "Walk around and you'll soon find one. Take care and goodbye."

"Hey, I wanna—!" Nick started saying, but the LOTUS's voice was already gone from his head, its departure marked by a series of rapidly fading echoes like the footsteps of a fleeing child.

Nick stood and stared, wondering in what direction to begin his search. The sheer number of books around him was mindboggling. Even before he'd begun it looked like his search for a spell to get him out of here might take forever.

And what did the voice say again? That God's angels took away the Book of Atrocities? So, right from the start, Drake's mad quest was for nothing? All that murder and bloodshed was for absolutely nothing?

Nick now began suspecting that that rotting, horrible monster that Drake Melville had called God might just have been another ordinary human visitor to the LOTUS, one who'd been transformed into that decaying tentacled atrocity and driven insane by what he'd learned in this timeless place.

And now it's my turn, Nick thought, staring in horror at the endless shelves of evil volumes facing him.

The End.

ABOUT THE AUTHOR

Wol-vriey is Nigerian, and quite tall.

He believes there actually are things that go bump in the night.

He writes horror fiction—for adults only, please. And also some surrealist stuff.

Wol-vriey blogs at: *http://odditytfarm.wordpress.com*

WOL-VRIEY

BIZARRO AND TRANSGRESSIVE FICTION

BOSTON POSH (BUD MALONE #1)

In 2028 AD, the USA is a nation ravaged by hungry dragons and dinosaurs. In Boston, Massachusetts, private eye Bud Malone is hired to rescue a kidnapped heiress. But nothing is as it seems.

Malone works to unravel a tangled web involving Boston Chinatown, a 200-year-old woman with a 9-year-old body, white robots, a human-liver-eating psychopath, a golem, a porcelain dragon, and a snake goddess with a crush on him. There's also a woman obsessed with chicken sex. Then Malone meets Posh Lane, a gorgeous call girl who's desperate to quit her pimp.

Romantic sparks ignite between Posh and Malone, but Posh's past suddenly catches up with her in a BIG way. To save Posh, Malone agrees to run a quest for Earth's new rulers, the Forks. But, Malone has no idea that agreeing to the Fork's odd request will send him on the weirdest trip he's ever been on in his life.

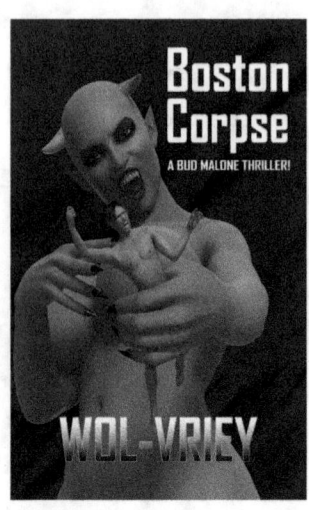

BOSTON CORPSE (BUD MALONE #2)

MAGIC CAN BE MURDER! - Drag queen Lucy Tang is back in Boston, and is hell-bent on settling her vindetta against casino owner Sookie Ling. And suddenly, Bud Malone, PI, has the case of his life to resolve.

When Boston's robot police force are baffled by a mind transfer case, they come to Malone for help. The one person who can likely help Malone out here is the witch Soledad Bathory. But Soledad seems to know a lot more than she's telling him. It's a case not made easier when Malone meets Soledad's beautiful cousin, Josephine 'Slave' Bailey. Slave has her own plans for Malone, most of which involve teaching him BDSM and making him her new Master.

Oh, and Rick Rogers owes Sookie Ling a whole lot of money, a gambling debt that's going to be literally Hell to pay!

BOSTON CORPSE - Not your average detective novel!

Burning Bulb
PUBLISHING

WOL-VRIEY
BIZARRO AND TRANSGRESSIVE FICTION

BOSTON LUST (BUD MALONE #3)

"Bless it, Father, for she has sinned."

Seven murdered gay women, all their bodies completely drained of blood. All also with large parts of their bodies dissolved away like acid has been pumped into their veins.

Bud Malone has to find the female vampire preying on Boston's lesbian population.

Then Malone meets the beautiful Trudi Carmen and the case gets even more tangled. Trudi needs Malone's help in recovering a ring that's gone missing. But how in the world is one little black ring related to either the dead women or their killer?

Resolving this case will lead Malone deep into Lucy Tang's legacy—The Abstracta. And then to the city of Genesis.

Boston Lust—Just when you thought Bean Town was safe to visit again.

HELL DANCER

Six people find themselves trapped in Detention, a nightmare realm where the demonic Schoolmaster is hell-bent on reforming them . . . until they die.

Porn superstar Venus Deluxe came to Springfield, MA to party, and next found her life hanging by a thread. One wrong answer will mean her death.

Suspended BPD detective Tanya Rockford was trying to stop one kind of violence, but found a terrifying another. With her and her companion's lives hanging in the balance, it's going to take all of her courage and resourcefulness to escape this hell she's stumbled into.

Porn stud Chad Cannon has made a career from his ten-inch penis. Here in Detention, however, it's his brains that matter. He'll soon be hoping all the pot he's smoked over the years hasn't completely messed up his memory.

The three students, Sherri, Jordan, and Mike? They were all just in the wrong place at the right time. Will anyone survive Detention? The evil Schoolmaster doesn't plan on letting that happen . . .

Burning Bulb
PUBLISHING

WOL-VRIEY
BIZARRO AND TRANSGRESSIVE FICTION

VAGINA MUNDI

Rachel Risk is a professional thief with super-strong hair that can stretch like tentacles to manipulate objects. Ashley Status has both a digitally augmented brain, and 'muscle-purses' in her arms and legs in which she stores inflatable objects—cars, guns, rocket launchers, etc.

When Raye is framed as the fall girl in a jewel robbery, the pair flee Chicago's vengeful robot gangsters and take refuge in the Hotel Bizarre, where the gorgeous 'vagina singer,' Femina, is performing for a week.

But the Hotel Bizarre is even stranger than its name suggests, and very soon Raye and Ash are involved in an deadly adventure, a struggle for survival the likes of which they'd never imagined possible—with loads of deviant sex, drugs, music, and violence at every turn. And just what is the old woman in the skin desert really doing with all those cats glued to her walls?

VAGINA MUNDI—a Bizarro Hymn in praise of WOMAN!

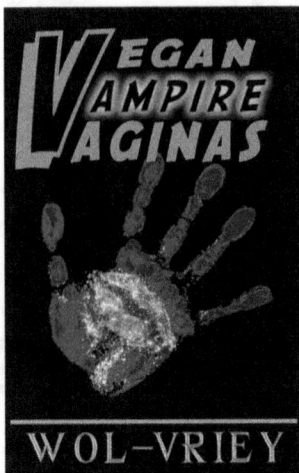

VEGAN VAMPIRE VAGINAS

The biggest bank heist in US history. And Tom Palmer can't remember pulling it off. And no, this isn't your standard case of amnesia. After a one-night-stand gone horribly wrong, Boston salesman Tom Palmer wakes up with a vagina implanted in his left hand. Then his day gets worse.

Tom is transported across space-time to a nightmare version of Boston, one where the Bizarro virus has transformed half the population into cannibals. Worst of all, Tom discovers that in this new Boston, he's the infamous gangster Pussypalm, wanted for robbing the Federal Reserve Bank of Boston a year ago. He also learns that the vagina in his hand is prophetic, i.e. it talks . . . after sex.

With 130 people left dead during his bank heist and six billion dollars missing, Tom knows he's living on borrowed time. It is in his best interests not to remember anything. Because once he does . . .

Burning Bulb
PUBLISHING

WOL-VRIEY
BIZARRO AND TRANSGRESSIVE FICTION

VEGAN ZOMBIE APOCALYPSE

In the post-apocalypse worlderness, zombies rule the earth. They're allergic to meat, and brains literally make them explode. Zombies now eat blood potatoes, parasitic tubers grown in the flesh of humancows corralled in maximum security farms. Two fugitives meet in the ancient ruins of Texas. The first is Soil 15-f, a womancow who's escaped her farm a week before she's due to be killed and her blood potato crop harvested. The second fugitive is Able Kane, former head necros food technician, now sentenced to death for heresy. But Soil is no ordinary humancow.

Unknown to herself, she's the vegan zombie agricultural revolution, and the zombies desperately want her back. And the necros equally desperately want Able Kane dead. He's fled with a forbidden discovery which will reshape the world for the worse if used. And Able is just hardheaded/misguided enough to use it.

MELANIE NEMESIS CATCHPOLE

In Springfield, Massachusetts, Melanie Catchpole is hired to fetch back a magic teddy bear worth millions of dollars from a warehouse across town. Problem is, the warehouse is down in Springfield's O-Zone—that totally weird sector of the city where Bizarro fell to Earth. The 'O' is a fairytale land, a place where dreams and nightmares literally live and breathe..

Worse still, the gingers—mutant cannibals—prowl the O. The gingers have already eaten everyone else Melanie's employers sent to get back the magic teddy bear.

Accompanied by the handsome but ruthless Doug Fisher (who she finds sexy but doesn't dare entrust her heart to), Melanie enters the O-Zone. Melanie and Doug are instantly caught up in an adventure they'd never have believed credible even if written as fiction . . . and Melanie's used to experiencing the very weird as the norm.

And now, additionally, there's a mystery to unravel: What does the dark, freezing-cold being called The Fixer want with Mary, the barkeep's daughter?

Burning Bulb
PUBLISHING

WOL-VRIEY

BIZARRO AND TRANSGRESSIVE FICTION

BIG TROUBLE IN LITTLE ASS

From Bizarro master storyteller Wol-vriey comes a truly weird western tale that will leave you awe-struck and on the edge of your seat...

In the town named Little Ass, tight-assed prostitute Rosa overhears a gunslinger's plans to assassinate rancher Edison Bennett. Once the badass Bennett learns of the plot, he ensures there'll be hell to pay for any attempt on his life!

Yes, it's going to take all of gunslinger Jude's shooting prowess, his eclectic collection of strange firearms, a trusty horse that requires an owners' manual, and the help of the lovely and invigorating Nell (who's EXTREMELY odd when the going gets weird), to survive the Bizarro hell that Edison Bennett unleashes in order to hold onto the land that he'd stolen from Madam Zizi.

BIZARRO 101 (A BASIC PRIMER)

Welcome to the strange place:

A collection of 37 flash fiction stories designed to introduce one to the Bizarro/New Weird Genre.

Weird, dreamy, nightmarish, absurd, sad, surreal, humorous . . . this collection of tales is all this and more.

***

"This primer is the very essence of any and all styles and types of Bizarro writing. Wol-vriey collects, distills, and bottles up these 37 tiny stories for your sensory enjoyment. This is an absolute must-read for anyone new to the genre, because it demonstrates the scope of what Bizarro is, and what it can be."
       –Teresa Pollack, Bizarro commentator and blogger

Burning Bulb
PUBLISHING

WOL-VRIEY
BIZARRO AND TRANSGRESSIVE FICTION

Dr. Orgasm

Courtney Taylor is young, intelligent, beautiful, and successful. She also has a boyfriend who loves her deeply. The problem is, no matter what Courtney does, she can't climax during sex.

When Florence Rigid's communist forces destroy the city of Metaphor, Courtney and her friends Teresa, Highball, Miki, and Heather are cast into the midst of a quest to find the only person able to save the land of Innuendo—Dr. Carol Orgasm, wanted by the communists for developing the O-Pill, a wonder drug that grants women sexual ecstasy on demand.

The communists will do anything to get their hands on the O-Pill and prevent its reaching the millions of Innuendo's women. But Courtney desperately wants that pill too. And so it's now a race between Courtney and the communists to find Dr. Orgasm first.

And Courtney has no choice but to win this race. She must win it: For her own orgasm . . . and for the freedom of female sexuality everywhere.

PUSSY TRANSMISSION

Pussy Transmission were the most decadent Pop Art ensemble of the 90's. Led by the beautiful painter Isis Lynch, the trio revolutionized the art world. Then suddenly, without explanation, Pussy Transmission vanished into historical obscurity. Now, twenty years later, three women come to Lynch Place. Lily and Nina are journalists desperate to interview Isis Lynch. Raven, on the other hand, wants to find her boyfriend, who's gone missing inside Isis's house. Raven's worried—she's heard that Pussy Transmission broke up because Isis began dabbling in black magic . . . with devastating results. All three women will shortly wish they'd never left home. Particularly once the rats in Lynch Place start warning them that they're going to die . . . and Raven meets Betty Butcher, the bouncy supernatural psycho who's intent on chopping her into bits. Pussy Transmission, Baby! Just because . . .

Burning Bulb
PUBLISHING

WOL-VRIEY
BIZARRO AND TRANSGRESSIVE FICTION

GIRLS ARE NOT SMILING
Welcome To The Road Trip From Hell

Pagan is demon-possessed.

Lori is suicidal.

Britt is just terminally pissed off.

Meet three young Boston women on the run from the law, each with problems that will fuse into more than the sum of their individual parts, becoming a holocaust of sex and violence and terror, a literal rain of blood and horror and gore and evil.

And if that wasn't already bad enough, Pagan's pet demon is slowly transforming her into something both unspeakable and unholy. Truly, these girls aren't smiling.

BLUE NIGHTMARES
Consummate EVIL is coming. It is relentless and unavoidable. It is Blue.

Jessica Schreiber is seeing things. Very horrible things. Since arriving in Raynham for what should have been a relaxing vacation, she's been seeing *The Big Blue*.

Jessica is smelling things too—dead and rotting things that she can't see. She is sure those dead and rotting things are dead people. Lots of dead people.

Jessica's worst nightmares will soon become her reality. Her reality will soon become a terrifying nightmare.

The tentacled residents of the House of Death have a lot that they wish to show Jessica Schreiber. They have a lot that they wish to tell her. But will she survive long enough to learn their lessons?

Burning Bulb
PUBLISHING

WOL-VRIEY
BIZARRO AND TRANSGRESSIVE FICTION

BRAINCHEW

It was supposed to be a simple jewel heist, but it went badly wrong. Chuck got shot and died.

Lance hid his friend's corpse in the Pleasant Street Cemetery. But that was a big mistake—there was something undead, something extremely hungry . . . something eXXXtremely horrible, buried in the Pleasant Street Cemetery.

And Lance had just woken it up.

They called the monster Brainchew because it ate brains. Human brains. And it preferred those brains fresh from the heads . . . of the living.

And now it was awake again, Brainchew planned on feeding big-time tonight. Oh hell yes, it did.

BRAINCHEW 2: OUT OF THEIR HEADS

After Tiff Hooper recognizes Josh Penham, the man who abducted her and kept her in his basement and abused her, she brings her three friends to Raynham for a night of well-deserved revenge on him.

Only things don't go according to plan.

It is never a good idea to leave a corpse in Raynham's Pleasant Street Cemetery. You run the very real risk of awakening what lies underground there. And that thing—Brainchew—is more horrible and more evil than anything the average mind conceives of even in its worst nightmares.

Brainchew is back! And this time the monster is extra-hungry. But there are plenty of delicious human brains about tonight, and Brainchew intends to eat them all before dawn.

Burning Bulb
PUBLISHING

WOL-VRIEY
BIZARRO AND TRANSGRESSIVE FICTION

DARIA: AN EROTIC NIGHTMARE

Even the best laid women can go wrong.

Daria Simpson is HUNGRY. She's HUNGRY for sex and bloodshed and death.

Shelly Parker just wanted to have a threesome with her boyfriend Craig and her best friend Erica. Everything was shaping up nicely for their weekend of sexual fun and games, until they stopped at the creepy Crossway Diner and met Daria.

From the moment they met Daria, EVERYTHING went wrong for them; and it went wrong in the most horrific and terrifying of ways!

Daria: Paranormal service has been resumed.

WET BONES

Greg is about learning the hard way that you don't mess with Aunt Grace.

Nine completely fleshless skeletons recovered in the Massachusetts woods. Two detectives on the trail of a horrible, hungry monster.

Broken-hearted Allie Jackson has a date with a creature from Hell.

Things are about to get well out of hand for everyone, and in horrifying, terrifying ways they don't expect.

Burning Bulb
PUBLISHING

WOL-VRIEY
BIZARRO AND TRANSGRESSIVE FICTION

MR. UGLY

When a rotting corpse appears and starts butchering Raynham's youths, there's really only one question that needs answering:

Is this faceless and rotting monster Peter Howard, or isn't it?

Problem is, Peter Howard died 15 years ago. So how can he possibly be back from the dead and murdering people with such relentless and incredible brutality?

Peter's mother Malicia, who's just been released from the lunatic asylum may have the answers to the crazy puzzle, but the two detectives investigating the deaths don't even know the right questions to ask her yet.

BRUTAL

Jane Winters is 28 years old.

She works as a checkout cashier in a department store. She's an attractive woman with a winning personality. She has both a photographic memory and an I.Q. of 189.

She's met the man of her dreams.

But she's also a cannibal with a unique and very scary mode of operation.

The group known as TULIP (The Urban Legend Investigation People) are out to either prove or disprove the legend of Insane Jane.

But have TULIP bitten off more than they can chew?

Burning Bulb
PUBLISHING

WOL-VRIEY
BIZARRO AND TRANSGRESSIVE FICTION

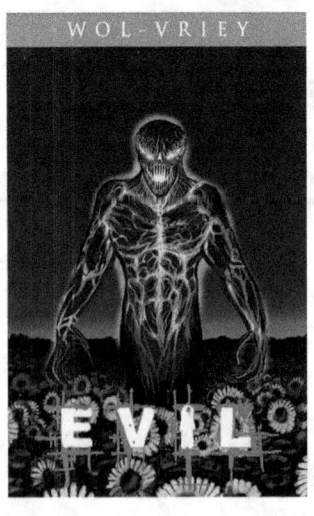

EVIL

The Evil began the week before Sylvia Stewart's 30th birthday.

Cathy Higgins died.

The Bargainer resurrected Cathy . . . for a price.

The price? Cathy's father Ronan had to plant some seeds for him.

But these were no ordinary seeds the Bargainer gave to Ronan Higgins. These were seeds from Hell: seeds which required human flesh as both soil and fertilizer.

And meanwhile, the unsuspecting Sylvia Stewart went ahead with the plans for her birthday party, which was to be held on Ronan Higgins' sunflower farm . . .

666

Ohio's State Route 666 stretches 14.7 miles between Zanesville and Dresden.

Most days, it's just a normal road with a funny name.

But for six minutes on the 6th of June each year, Route 666 becomes a gateway to somewhere else . . . a gateway to Hell.

Each year 13 unfortunates get trapped in the 666 underworld, with no way to get back home.

This year though, things are going to be very different. For one thing, there are currently a whole lot of turbulent human emotions at play in the underworld. And also . . . the psycho Al Gore is just about completing his collection of human heads.

And . . . what the hell is a church doing in Hell, of all places?

Burning Bulb
PUBLISHING

WOL-VRIEY
BIZARRO AND TRANSGRESSIVE FICTION

THE CLEAVERMAN

It began as a joke, a gag to pass the time that turned deadly. One rainy August night in Raynham, MA, nine friends jokingly invoke the evil phantom butcher called the Cleaverman.

These nine friends get a whole lot more than they ever bargained for. Because there's only one way to return the deadly Cleaverman back to the darkness he came from, and that is to solve his riddle, which starts: "Tell me the name of John Cleaverman's wife . . ."

And human beings being what we are, even with the Cleaverman out to butcher them all, our nine friends still manage to stir A WHOLE LOT of human misbehavior into the deadly mix.

At the rate they're going, it'll be a wonder if anyone survives THE CLEAVERMAN at all.

PERVERSE

When 21-year-old Heather Forrest accompanies three of her friends on a weekend trip up to Vermont, she has no idea what she's getting into.

Because, during a brief stop in the western Massachusetts woods, the girls get kidnapped and things go rapidly downhill from there. Soon Heather and her friends are fighting for their lives, fighting to survive the most perverted and impossible situation imaginable. And meanwhile, Hank Rollins is also in the woods, hunting the unholy monster that killed his wife and son . . . and he's hunting it with live human bait.

Oh yes, there will be blood. And there will be terror and buckets of gore also. And truly horrible atrocities will happen. Most definitely so.

Burning Bulb
PUBLISHING

WOL-VRIEY
BIZARRO AND TRANSGRESSIVE FICTION

THE VIRGIN

10 million dollars in prize money. 1000+ video cameras, lots of deadly weapons, 10 Suitors, 5 Virgins & 3 Hours . . . to keep your hymen intact.

Hailey Osborne wants to sell her virginity for a hundred thousand dollars. But then she's made an offer she really can't refuse: how about competing to win ten million dollars in a no-holds-barred underground game show, where all she has to do is remain a virgin?

There's just two problems:
1. Four other women also want that prize money.
2. There's ten suitors all contesting to take Hailey and the other virgins' precious hymens . . . by any means necessary . . .

But hey, it's just for 3 hours, right? How hard can it possibly be ? Hailey Osborne is about to find out.

THE BOOK OF ATROCITIES

Bestselling author Drake Melville has been missing for three years now. Drake vanished after publishing The Bleeding Oysters, an epic novel that set new standards for depictions of sleaze and depravity and human monstrosity in popular fiction. On vanishing, however, Drake Melville left a message for everyone, saying he'd 'left town' to go work on his follow-up novel The Book of Atrocities. The problem was, no one could find Drake. It seemed like he'd vanished off the face of the Earth. And now, three years later, Drake has just sent messages to his ex-wife Liz, his current (and abandoned) wife Melody; and his younger sister Chloe . . . asking them to meet him in Raynham, MA. Drake says he's now completed The Book of Atrocities and is ready to present it to the world. But there's a whole lot that Liz, Melody, and Chloe Melville don't know about Drake's Book of Atrocities. And unfortunately they're on their way to find out those excruciatingly painful truths. Because, see, Drake Melville is a VERY EVIL man with a VERY EVIL plan . . .

Burning Bulb
PUBLISHING